# Witch Child

# Witch Child

## CELIA REES

SCHOLASTIC INC.

New York  Toronto  London  Auckland  Sydney
Mexico City  New Delhi  Hong Kong  Buenos Aires

Acknowledgment:
To Julia Griffiths Jones for her advice about quilts and
quilting, and for the interest she has shown in this book.

ISBN 0-439-46850-7

12 11 10 9 8 7 6 5 4 3                    2 3 4 5 6 7/0

Printed in the U.S.A.                40

First Scholastic printing, September 2002
This book was typeset in Centaur.

For Rachel

The following manuscript comes from a remarkable collection of documents termed "the Mary papers." Found hidden inside a newly discovered and extremely rare quilt from the colonial period, the papers seem to take the form of an irregularly kept journal or diary. All dates are guesswork, based on references within the text. The first entries are tentatively dated from March 1659. I have altered the original as little as possible, but punctuation, paragraphing, and spellings have been standardized for the modern reader.

Alison Ellman
Boston, MA

beginning

## 1. Early March 1659

*I am Mary*

I am a witch. Or so some would call me. "Spawn of the Devil," "Witch child," they hiss in the street, although I know neither father nor mother. I know only my grandmother, Eliza Nuttall; Mother Nuttall to her neighbors. She brought me up from a baby. If she knew who my parents are, she never told me.

"Daughter of the Erl King and the Elfen Queen, that's who you are."

We live in a small cottage on the very edge of the forest; Grandmother, me, and her cat and my rabbit.

*Lived.* Live there no more.

Men came and dragged her away. Men in black coats and hats as tall as steeples. They skewered the cat on a pike; they smashed the rabbit's skull by hitting him against the wall. They said that these were not God's creatures but familiars, the Devil himself in disguise. They threw the mess of fur and flesh on to the midden and threatened to do the same to me, to her, if she did not confess her sins to them.

3

They took her away then.

She was locked in the keep for more than a week. First they "walked" her, marching her up and down, up and down between them for a day and a night until she could no longer hobble, her feet all bloody and swollen. She would not confess. So they set about to prove she was a witch. They called in a woman, a Witch Pricker, who stabbed my grandmother all over with long pins, probing for the spot that was numb, where no blood ran, the place where the familiars fed. The men watched as the woman did this, and my grandmother was forced to stand before their gloating eyes, a naked old lady, deprived of modesty and dignity, the blood streaming down her withered body, and still she would not confess.

They decided to "float" her. They had plenty of evidence against her, you see. Plenty. All week folk had been coming to them with accusations. How she had overlooked them, bringing sickness to their livestock and families; how she had used magic, sticking pins in wax figures to bring on affliction; how she had transformed herself and roamed the country for miles around as a great hare and how she did this by the use of ointment made from melted corpse fat. They questioned me, demanding, "Is this so?"

She slept in the bed next to me every night, but how do I know where she went when sleep took her?

4

It was all lies. Nonsense and lies.

These people accusing her, they were our friends, our neighbors. They had gone to her, pleading with her for help with beasts and children, sick or injured, a wife nearing her time. Birth or death, my grandmother was asked to be there to assist in the passage from one world to the next, for she had the skill—in herbs, potions, in her hands—but the power came from inside her, not from the Devil. The people trusted her, or they had until now; they had wanted her presence.

They were all there for the swimming, standing both sides of the river, lining the bridge, staring down at the place, a wide pool where the water showed black and deep. The men in tall hats dragged my grandmother from the stinking hole where they had been keeping her. They cross-bound her, tying her right toe to her left thumb and vice versa, making sure the cords were thin and taut. Then they threw her in. The crowd watched in silence, the only sound the shuffle of many feet edging forward to see what she would do.

"She floats!"

The chant started with just one person remarking, in a quiet voice almost of wonder, then it spread from one to another until all were shouting, like some monstrous howling thing. To float was a sure proof of guilt. They hooked her, pulling her back to shore like a bundle of old washing. They did not want her drowning, because that would deprive them of a hanging.

## 2.

*It is a cold day,* even for the early spring. White frost on the ground and green barely touching the trees, but folk come from far and near for the hanging. They crowd the market square worse than for a fair.

It is dangerous for me to be there. I see them glancing and whispering, "That's her, the granddaughter," "Daughter of the Devil, more like." Then they turn away, sniggering, hands covering their mouths, faces turning red at the lewd images they conjure in their own mind's eye. The evil is in themselves.

I should flee, get away. They will turn on me next unless I go. But where to? What am I to do? Lose myself. Die in the forest. I look around. Eyes, hard with hatred, slide from mine. Mouths twitch between leering and sneering. I will not run away into the forest, because that is what they want me to do.

I keep my eyes forward now, staring at the gallows. They have hammered away for a night and a day putting it up. You can smell the fresh-cut wood, even from where I stand at the back of the crowd.

What powers do they think we have, my grandmother and I? If she had real power, would she not be able to undo the locks to their stinking dungeon and fly through the air to safety? Would she not call up her master, Satan, to blast and shrivel them to dust and powder? And if *I* had any powers, any at all, I would destroy all these people, right here and now. I would turn them into a mass of fornicating toads. I would turn them into leprous blind newts and set them to eating themselves. I would cover their bodies with suppurating sores. I would curse them from generation to generation, down through the ages, so their children and their children's children bore gaggling half-wits. I would addle their heads, curdling, corrupting the insides of their skulls until their brains dripped from their noses, like bloody mucus. . . .

I was so lost in my curses that only the sudden silence of the crowd brought me back to what was about to happen. Black figures stood on the pale boards, silhouetted against the white of the sky: Witchfinder, Minister, Hangman. In the unexpected quiet, a sneeze sounded, loud. Obadiah Wilson's thin figure bent forward, suddenly convulsed. He took a handkerchief from his pocket and held it to his face as sneeze after sneeze racked him. When he took it away, the crowd drew breath. Blood bloomed thick and red on the snow-white linen. It was the only color on the whole platform.

My grandmother was brought forward for all to see. She was held, arms pinioned behind her, then pushed to the foot of the ladder that leaned against the gallows tree. She ignored the eyes on her, looking over the upturned heads, searching for me. Her eyes found mine and she smiled. Her glance went sideways to Obadiah Wilson, self-appointed Witchfinder, trying to staunch the blood pouring from his nostrils, and she nodded very slightly, as if to say well done. She nodded again to someone behind me.

That was the last I saw of her. The hangman stepped forward. He held a hood raised to cover her face, and at the same time a cloak closed around me. I was taken down one of the steep alleys leading from the market and was pushed into a waiting carriage just as I heard the crowd's roar.

3.

The woman sitting opposite me said not a word, nor I to her. She stared out the window, studying the passing scene while I studied her. She was obviously a lady, richly apparelled. Her cloak was soft dark wool fastened at the throat with a silver clasp and chain; her dress was green silk-velvet, the shifting shade of young beech leaves turning in a spring wind. Her hands were gloved, her fingers long and thin, and I could see beneath the soft leather the bulge of many rings. Her face was veiled. Black gauze as fine as mist obscured her features, but I could see enough to know that she was young and comely. Her skin was pale, and I could make out the shadowed jut of high cheekbones and the curve of finely molded lips. I could not see her eyes, and anyway, they were not upon me. They stared outward steadily.

If she was aware of my scrutiny, she showed no sign of it and made no comment as the coach rumbled on. I wondered if she stared out to look for robbers, for in these lawless times the roads are infested with roaming packs of sundry vagabonds and bands of soldiers left over from both armies. Though many are fearful to travel, my captor had made no attempt to hide her wealth.

She did not seem inclined to tell me who she was, and I did not ask her. In my mind an old rhyme began to chime. As we travelled onward, the wheels of the carriage took up the rhythm:

"In the town live witches nine: three in worsted, three in rags, and three in velvet fine. . . ."

*journey one*

## 4. March 1659

*The change in the motion* of the carriage woke me. I must have fallen asleep, my senses dulled by exhaustion and lulled by the constant swaying movement. I started up at the sound of horses' hooves clattering on cobblestones. Outside the day had darkened. I judged it to be late afternoon, although tall buildings crowded out the sky. The coachman called and the horses neighed in answer as the coach turned into a wide inn-yard.

"Where are we?"

My companion still said nothing, merely smiled beneath her veil and put one gloved finger to her lips. The coach had come to a halt. I drew back the leather curtain a little more to peer out. The coachman opened the door for my companion to step down. People came running: an ostler, reaching to hold the horses; the innkeeper, bowing, and his wife, dropping curtsies. Their eyes widened somewhat as my companion turned back to help me out, but they said nothing. It was as if we were expected. I stumbled slightly, my legs stiff from sitting so long and my head still rocking with the motion of the coach. The hand on mine tightened and did not let go.

We were shown to a spacious room, part bed-chamber, part parlor; obviously the best the inn could provide. The landlady brought food and drink: pewter

13

plates laden with stewed meat—mutton by the smell of it—wheaten bread and cheese, a mug of beer for me, and wine for my companion. Then she laid the food, bobbed her head at both of us, and left.

My companion ate little, just lifted her veil to sip her wine, crumbled some bread between her gloved fingers, and pushed the stew about on her plate. Perhaps the food was too rough for her taste. I was aware of her eyes upon me, that now I was the object of her study, but I did not look up until all the food was finished, the last smears of gravy wiped around with bread. Despite her scrutiny, and despite all the things that had happened to me, I had found that I was very hungry indeed.

"Are you sufficed?" Her thin fingers drummed the table.

I nodded.

"Is this room to your liking?"

I nodded again.

"Good." She stood up. "Now I must leave you. I have much to do. Annie, the landlady, will care for you. You will be safe with her; have no fear."

With that she left. I heard her outside the room, talking to the landlady and ordering a bath for me. This duly arrived—a great tub lined with linen, followed by maids bringing pitchers of steaming water. I had never even seen such a thing before, let alone been in one. At home—my eyes stung at the thought of it—at home we bathed in the river, if we bathed at all. The landlady came bustling in when all was ready and took charge of me. I was ordered to undress.

"That too," she said when I was down to my shift.

A maid collected my clothes and took them away with her.

"Where is she taking them?"

"To be burned."

"What am I to wear?"

"This until tomorrow." She had a long white linen gown over her arm.

I was left standing naked before her. My hand went to my neck. I wore a small leather pouch there, made for me by my grandmother. It contained things, special things, not to be seen by anyone. The hot blood rushed to my cheeks. I feared that I was undone.

"You are safe with me," she said quietly, as if she knew who I was and what I had come from. "Put it aside, and then into the tub with you."

Annie was a big woman with little black eyes set like currants in a round bun of a face. She rolled her sleeves to show forearms as thick as ham hocks, caught me in a farmer's grip, and began to scrub me clean. I had not thought myself especially dirty, not compared to most in our village anyway, but it took two changes of water before Annie was happy. My hair caused the most difficulty. It was tangled and knotted, snarling up in the comb so she had to shear hunks of it away.

15

Then she anointed me with a sharp-smelling concoction.

"Black alder bark boiled in vinegar," she replied when I questioned her. "You're as lousy as a beggar's dog."

She left that to soak in while she scrubbed away at the rest of me with lumpy balls of hard soap and bags of sweet herbs. Then she attacked my head again, with a finetoothed comb to remove all the nits and lice. It felt as though most of my hair was going with them and my scalp was near bleeding before she was satisfied. I sat in the tub until the water was cold and I was shivering. Finally she bade me get out and rubbed me pink and warm again inside a sheet of coarse linen.

"There." She held me at arm's length, her face red and sweating. She parted my hair and peered at my scalp and then looked me over from head to foot before pronouncing, "I think you'll do." She held the nightgown for me. "Into bed with you. I'll bring you up a posset." Her homely face creased in a smile. "You're quite a pretty one under all that dirt." Suddenly she hugged me. "Poor little maid. What's to become of you?"

The bath was cleared away, the dirty water emptied in a great *sloosh* out in the yard, and I was left alone. I took the candle and went over to the cracked and misted mirror that stood on top of a tall chest of drawers. Soapsuds and kind words had brought the tears stinging to my eyes. They stared back, red rimmed, the irises a black bordered, luminous gray flecked with yellow, gazing out of a face all pink and white and many shades paler than before. My hair fell down in thick cords, gray as ash bark, the tips drying to dull gold, the color of oak leaves in winter. It framed a countenance full of unfamiliar hollows and shadows. Perhaps it was the candle's flickering light, but I seemed to be looking into another's face, a stranger's face. The face of a woman, not a child.

A knock at the door made my eyes start wide as a deer's. It was the maid carrying my posset. The mess of bread was well-soaked in hot milk, generously flavored with brandy, honey, and spices. I stirred it with the horn spoon and ate it slowly, letting its warmth comfort me. I stayed curled up in a chair in front of the fire until the logs fell to red embers. Only then did I climb into bed.

I had never been in a bed like that one before. I had only known the little sleeping platform in the smoky loft of our one-room cottage, rough homespun blankets, straw-stuffed paillasse. This bed was heated by a brass pan full of coals, but that was no comfort. I missed my grandmother's warm bulk next to me. She was all that I knew, all that was dear. I'd loved her and she'd loved me. Now I was alone in the world. How would I do without her? My thoughts echoed the landlady: What would become of me? I turned my face into the feather bolster and clutched tight the woolen blanket and smooth white linen. I drew them about my head to muffle the sound as I wept.

## 5.

*I did not again see the woman* who had brought me here until on into the next evening. In the meantime Annie looked after me, feeding me and bringing new clothes: linen skirt, bodice and jacket, and a cap to cover my hair. Good material. Not the finest, but better than the rough homespun stuff that I was used to. Plain, dark colors. Sad colors.

My window had a good view of the yard. I turned the chair and sat there in my new clothes, looking out. I had been told to keep to my room, so spying was my only amusement. Just as the light was fading I saw her coach turn into the yard. She got down but told the coachman to wait. An ostler came out to feed and water the horses, but he did not take them from their traces. We were to travel on together, or so I thought.

"Quite the little Puritan," she said as she came in through the door. "Let me see you." She came over to my place at the window. "You will do well enough. At least you look the part."

"Well enough for what?"

I looked at her, comparing my plain clothes with her rich attire, and suddenly knew that I would not be going with her.

She seated herself in a chair opposite me. "We live in difficult times. Lord Protector Cromwell is dead. His son's rule will not last much longer. Charles will come from exile and we will have a king again. Already the people are clamoring for him and there are plots aplenty to get him here. Then who knows what will happen?"

I looked at her, trying to see through her veil to search her face for clues as to what this had to do with me.

"There are those who do not want to stay here, in this country. Puritans, separatists, people who fear that their faith will no longer be tolerated. They are leaving for a new life. In America."

Puritans. Separatists. I looked down at myself.

"And I am to join them?"

She nodded.

*"America!"*

I would not have been more astonished if she had told me that I was bound for the realm of Faerie. In fact, that seemed more real to me. I had visited it often enough through my grandmother's stories, but a new world across the ocean? I had heard of it. I knew that such a place existed, but I had never thought to visit it, and I had no way of imagining what it could be like there.

"Yes, America. They take ship soon. You will go from here to meet them in Southampton."

"Why?"

"It is not safe for you here. My husband was a soldier in Cromwell's army. Some of their number served under him. They are good people; they will care for you."

"What shall I tell them? About myself; who I am." I bit my lip. They were bound to be curious, and Puritans do not like witches. This seemed a dangerous course to take.

"You are Mary Newbury," she went on quickly. "An orphan. Father, a soldier, killed at the Battle of Worcester, fighting in Cromwell's army. Your mother, dead of a wasting sickness. Grandmother too feeble to care for you."

"Where am I from?"

"Your mother was on the road until she fell ill. Your grandmother lived in a little village, no more than a hamlet, outside Warwick. Near to where she really lived, but not too near. You were only with your grandmother a short while. That is the story you will tell, though I doubt that you will be questioned too closely. They are departing the country and have concerns of their own. You should slip among them without much notice. I will give you a letter of introduction. Give it to John Rivers, along with your fare."

"But why must I go with them? Why can I not stay with you?"

She shook her head. "That would be impossible."

"Why?"

"I am in danger myself."

I did not believe her. To me she seemed untouchable.

"It is true, I do assure you. My husband put his name to the old King's death warrant. All who signed will be arrested as soon as the new King returns." She sighed, and when she spoke again her voice was quiet and bitter. "He might as well have signed his own."

I did not know what to say. Her husband must be a man of very great importance to be involved in such high affairs of state. This made her even grander in my eyes, but not that alone silenced me. My grandmother was no Royalist. She'd been on the side of Parliament in the War, but she'd seen the killing of an anointed king as a dread sin. To be married to one with *that* blood on his hands filled me with awe.

"If that be so, why do you not flee to America instead of me?"

She shook her head again. "It cannot be. My husband will not leave; he would see it as cowardice, and I must stand by him. Anyway, he would not be safe there. He will not be safe anywhere once Charles is on the throne. It will be time to go soon," she added, abruptly switching to practical matters. "Gather your things."

I looked around, at a loss; I was standing in all I possessed. She seemed to remember this.

"Ah, yes. Your box is already loaded. I have tried to anticipate your needs." She handed me a purse. "Here is money for your fare, or should you wish to purchase anything else. There are rogues everywhere, so keep it close and guard it well. John Rivers and his party wait to take ship at an inn in Southampton. The carter knows where. He will take you there. Give this to Rivers as soon as you arrive."

She thrust the letter at me and turned abruptly, as if to go.

"Wait! Wait, madam!" I took her sleeve to restrain her. "There are some things that I must know."

"Well?"

Her voice had retained its cold formality. The questions dried in my throat, but I did not let go. I would not let her leave. Not until I knew.

"Why?" I said, finally. "Why me?"

"I owe a great debt to Eliza Nuttall, the woman you call Grandmother. She was my nurse. As a child I held her in great affection. I was as close to her as you are. Were," she corrected. "Later she helped me in a time of trouble, when no other could. She rendered me a service and now it is my turn. Over the years, I tried to help her, make sure she was comfortable."

How had Eliza Nuttall lived so well with no man to keep her? That had long provoked suspicion.

"But my husband is a soldier and latterly a politician; following him took me far away. I came when I heard of her trouble, but I was too late—too late to prevent . . ." She stopped for a moment to collect herself. "The only way I can repay her now is through you. Now haste, there is no time to waste."

She came toward me and lifted her veil. She took me into her arms in the briefest of embraces. She smelled of flowers. For a moment I breathed the sweet haunting scent of roses, then she let me go.

"Here. Take this as a token and talisman."

She took a ring from her finger. A purple stone, flat cut, engraved with the initial *E* at the center. My fingers closed around it. The gold weighed heavy in my hand.

I looked into her eyes and saw my own staring back, the same peculiar shade, pale gray, flecked with yellow, rimmed with black. Now I knew the nature of her debt; it had weighed on her conscience for fourteen years. I was looking into the eyes of my mother, and I knew that I would never see her again.

## 6

*The carter picked me up* as if I weighed nothing. He was a big man, hunched over, with long arms stretching down. He was wrapped up in layers of clothing and wore a big black hat, shapeless and greasy, low over his forehead. He put me on the little bench above the horses, then swung himself up next to me with surprising agility. The horses pulled in their traces, impatient to get started. The heavy animals stamped their great feet, snorting and blowing, their breath showing like plumes. I pulled my cloak about me, glad that it was thick wool and of good quality, for the air was chill.

The carter sniffed the air and muttered, "Frost tonight, you see if there ent."

He wound his scarf tighter and whipped up the horses, and we were clattering out of the inn yard and into the cobbled street.

Soon the cobbles ended and the thick wheels jolted over the rutted track that was the road south. I said little to the carter; he even less to me. I felt small next to him, and lonely, full of doubt and uncertainty. I could see no end to the journey I was starting.

I must have fallen asleep, for I woke to find us crossing a vast open plain.

"Them's Merlin's Stones, them is."

The carter waved his whip toward huge stones looming to the right of us, rearing up out of the close-cropped grass. I stared, transfixed; this must be the great Temple of the Winds. My grandmother had told me about it. A circle of stones, much, much greater than any other, built far to the south of our home. Such places are sacred to those who live by the Old Religion. At certain times of the year my grandmother had set off for some stones that lay a day's journey or so from where we lived. She never told me what went on there or who else attended, and I knew better than to ask her. The rituals practiced there were mysteries, the celebrants known only to one another.

Soon the great stones faded. Darkness drew in on either side, and there was only the road unwinding like a white thread in the moonlight.

Beyond that all was black.

### 7.

*I had never seen the sea,* but even before the carter's brawny arm shook me, I felt a difference in the air, damp against my cheek and smelling of salt and fishy decay, and I heard the cry of the gulls, like mocking laughter. I opened my eyes to white curling mist. The masts and rigging of tall ships showed through it like bare branches in winter. The cart rumbled along the quayside on its iron-rimmed wheels, and all around were the suck and slap of water, the creaking of timbers, the grinding of ships rubbing together. I wondered which of them would take me to America.

Puritans are early risers. The day was scarce past first light, but they were already breaking their fast in the inn's cavernous parlor. I stood at the door, reluctant to enter, listening to the murmur of voices, the rattle of dishes, food being chewed. The moment weighed heavy upon me. As soon as they noticed me, my life would be changed entirely. I wanted to run away, but where could I run to? The carter had already left to make his other deliveries. I had no place in the world to go.

The children noticed me first. They were good and dutiful: eating their food quietly, only speaking when spoken to, but their eyes were moving all the time, darting this way and that, alert to the chance of distraction. A row of little ones looked at me, then at one another. One of them pulled the sleeve of an older girl, older than me, about seventeen, whom I took to be her sister. She, in her turn, regarded me with large grave eyes before dabbing her lips with her napkin and touching the arm of the man sitting next to her.

"Father . . ."

The man looked up and saw me standing in the doorway. He continued to chew his food carefully.

Then he swallowed and stood up. He came toward me, a man of above-average height, his light brown hair graying, hanging straight to his shoulders. I judged him to be a farmer. His face was leathery from outdoor work, the skin round his eyes crinkled at the sides from squinting at the weather, and the hand that shook mine was callused across the palm.

"You must be Mary. Welcome, child. You have been expected."

His eyes crinkled further in a smile, and as he looked down at me, I saw that his face, although hard and grooved with lines, was kindly.

"Thank you, sir," I replied, and dropped what I knew of a curtsy. "And you are?"

"John Rivers." His voice was deep, and the words came drawn out and slow, different from where I lived.

"This, then, is for you."

I handed him the letter I had been given. He read it and nodded before tucking it inside his jerkin.

"Are you hungry? Come. Sit. Eat."

He led me back to his table. The children shuffled along the bench to make room for me. His wife ladled porridge from a pot over the fire, moving slowly as if her back pained her. I guessed her seven months with child, perhaps more than that, although little showed under her bulky clothes. The girl who first saw me filled a mug with ale and then turned away to help her mother. I remembered to mutter a prayer of thanks, in part for the food but also for my own deliverance.

As I ate I felt curious eyes on me. I observed back from under my lashes. As yet no face stood out from another. They appeared as similar as the lumps in the porridge in front of me. I estimated about twenty families in all. Folk of a middling sort—none very rich; none very poor. A mix of farmers and tradesmen, all dressed in the dark, sober clothes that mark them as Puritans. I had no clue as to what type. They could belong to any one of a multitude of sects, each one with their own set of beliefs. It would not do to say the wrong thing. I would have to listen carefully and take my lead from what I heard.

They soon lost interest in me and went back to eating and talking among themselves. I could see strain on their faces, hear worry in the low muttering voices. These people had suffered, like folk everywhere, their lives thrown into confusion time and again by war, bad harvests, poor prices, lack of trade. Peace and prosperity go together; that's what my grandmother used to say, and the country had seen neither for too many years. Most folk just put up with misfortune, taking it as their lot, but these were different. Disappointed, disillusioned, doubting what was to come. Bitterness had grown in them until it was strong enough to drive them across an ocean. But what would happen then? They were as anxious as I was. I saw my own fears reflected all about me.

"On your own, young'un?"

I turned and saw a woman smiling at me. She was past her middle years. The hair tucked beneath her cap was streaked with gray, and her skin was wrinkled as a winter apple, but her eyes were bright and sharp.

"That I am." I tried to muster a smile, but this crowded room, all the families together, had made me feel more lonely than ever. "My name is Mary."

"I'm Martha. Martha Everdale." She put out her hand to shake mine, like a man. Her fingers were strong, her palm toughened by work to the hardness of polished oak. "I'm alone too. Husband dead. Children along with him." She looked away to the distance for a moment, as if into some time past, and then back at me again, examining me closely, head cocked to one side, as though making up her mind. "We could make a good pair, I reckon. You can travel along a' me."

When we had finished breakfast, Martha took me upstairs to a large room where many of the families were sleeping. There was hardly space to move among their goods and the makeshift beds.

"You can stow your goods along a' mine." She looked around. "We're all from the same place, more or less. Same town, same church. We follow our pastor, Reverend Johnson. Him and the other church members who left years ago. We were to follow soon after, but the War made everything uncertain. We were content to bide for a time, but now the will is to go."

"'The will'?"

"Of the Congregation. 'Tis important that all should be together, and I go to find my sisters. They're all I have left."

"How will you know where to find them?"

"Trust to the Lord's guidance." She spoke simply, as though this was a truth too obvious to question. "Now." She smiled down at me. "Tell me, Mary, where are you from?"

"Warwickshire. A little village."

"No one left there?"

I shook my head and lowered my eyes as if tears threatened to spill. I was careful not to say much, but she did not ask about my family or how I came to be here. She just cupped her hand under my chin and looked into my face. Her green eyes seemed to see clear into me. It was as if she did not need to question me. She knew already.

She took a lock of hair from my brow, tucking it under my cap. Her fingers smelled of juniper and made my cheek tingle. She had a healer's touch.

"You are with a friend now. Never fret."

I stayed with her as she moved among the others, making herself useful, talking to this one and that one, introducing me to the company. She let me hide behind her chatter. The less said, the better. Lies are not rooted in the mind in the way truth is. Some thought me a relation of Martha's, a niece or a grand-daughter. We let them think what they would.

It is not uncommon for orphan boys and girls to be taken to America. Not infants or babes in arms, but sturdy boys, and girls nearing womanhood. The colony needs brawny arms and strong backs to fell trees and farm, and a good supply of wives and moth-ers to populate the new land. There will be others like me, attached to families—with them but not of them. It seemed to me an awkward position, like a servant but not so. All in all, I am glad that I found Martha or, rather, that she found me.

As we went about I watched the other girls my age, observing how to behave, how to be the perfect little Puritan maid. Rebekah Rivers, the girl who first saw me, made a good model, for she is quiet and helps her mother. Others, I noticed, were not so demure. They giggle together and flirt with the inn servants and don't help anyone at all.

It was not until evening drew in that I was able to examine the box that accompanied me here. It was not big, but handsomely made, and carved with my ini-tials, M. N. My heart beat hard when I opened it, wondering what I would find. The letter I hoped for was at the top.

*Mary,*

> *I hope the box pleases you and that you make good use of what it contains. It is no good wishing for what was not to be. Fate took us apart and has contrived to keep us so. You are ever in my thoughts, that you must know, and you will not be alone, however you think otherwise, wherever you go. I could write more, fill pages, but I see no point in it.*
>
> *Do not doubt that I love you.*
>
> *Farewell and may God be with you and keep you.*
>
> *E.*

My hands shook while I read it. I sat for a moment, staring at it as though these few lines of writing could reveal the woman I would never know. Then I put the letter aside. No good crying over milk shed; that's what my grandmother would have said.

I turned to examine the rest of the box. This is what I found: clothes—several changes; spare sets of linen; a length of good cloth; sewing things—needles, threads, a silver thimble; a sheathed knife; a pewter plate; another knife; a spoon and a fork to eat with. Basic necessaries. It could have been packed by a maid.

At the bottom were ink, quill, and a deal of paper, folded to make a book. I seized on this, turning the leaves, hoping that here I would find answers to ease my heart. I put them back, my disappointment turning to anger. If it was a jest, I did not see the humor. Every page was blank.

But I use the ink and quill to begin my Journal now. Many here are writing them, to record the commencement of their Great Adventure. I resolved to do the same. For I do feel alone, very alone, whatever she may say.

8.

*The ship was to set sail* on the morning of my arrival, but the mist came in with the tide, bringing a dead calm. It lingered all day, smothering everything like a great fleece. The men went down to the dock and the women peered into the street. Ships can be confined for a week or more, becalmed like this or kept in port by contrary winds. With each hour anxiety increases. These Puritans are careful people, and every shilling spent here is a shilling less to spend in the New Land.

As night comes on, the fog lies as thick as ever. The captain of the vessel had come to the inn, his fleshy face as long as a fiddle, to meet with the church Elders in worried consultation. They are inclined to say that there is no help, that it is God's Providence, His Will, and they have declared tomorrow a day of solemn humiliation, of preaching, prayer, and fasting. The captain left then, gloomier than ever, cursing under his breath, wanting to know what damned good it all will do.

9.

*This morning, breakfast was replaced* by prayers, and they were led by a man whom I have not seen before. He is young for a preacher, not out of his twenties, tall and very thin. He wore a rounded hat, and from under it hung whitish hair, tinged with yellow, straight as flax. The tabs at his throat proclaim him an ordained minister, and he is treated with deference by the Elders.

I whispered to Martha, asking who he was.

"Elias Cornwell. Reverend Johnson's nephew. He ent been with us long. Come from Cambridge."

He is young, but he stands with his shoulders hunched and his back bent, like an old man. Scholar's stance, Martha calls it. His black clothes hang loose on him, and his bony wrists thrust out from his sleeves as if his coat is too small for him. His long pale hands fluttered like a spider over the pages of the Bible, the fingers inked from nail to knuckle. He found his place, looked over the heads bowed in front of him, and prepared to speak.

Elias Cornwell reminds me of a ferret. His face is white to milkiness, with pinched features gathering into a thin pointed nose. The tip is pink and square ended. I keep expecting it to twitch.

He removed his hat and cast pale eyes over us, catching mine before I could lower them. Frown lines marked his high sloping forehead, and I thought I saw that sensitive nose twitch as if scenting an interloper. I hurriedly studied the rough floorboards beneath my feet.

He marked his place in the Bible, but he did not read. The text he had chosen was learned by heart. His speaking voice was a surprise to me. Deep and full despite his frail frame, it filled the small hall.

"We are God's chosen people. His purpose for us is clear. 'I will appoint a place for my people Israel, and will plant them, that they may dwell in a place of their own, and move no more; neither shall the children of wickedness afflict them anymore, as beforetime . . .'"

He was quoting from the Second Book of Samuel. Grandmother made sure that I was well versed in biblical matters.

His rich voice rang out over the congregation. Heads nodded slightly in response to his words; shoulders and backs braced and relaxed with the rhythm of his preaching. He spoke a belief that was shared by all.

"If we have transgressed, if we have strayed in any way from God's purpose, we must beg His forgiveness. We must pray . . ."

I listened for a while—there was much to admire —in his eloquence—but as the hourglass turned I found my attention straying. I am used to lengthy preaching and praying, and well practiced in seeming to be devout. But I thought my own thoughts, all the while trying to keep my mind away from the aching discomfort spreading up my legs from the hard floor and the long standing.

My grandmother always attended church, tramping in all weathers the path from our cottage in the woods to the village and taking me with her, even though she did not believe a word of what was said and it was four miles there and four miles back. She went every Sunday, even after they had sent the vicar packing and burned his robes, taken mallets to the statues of the saints and the Virgin, smashed the colored glass in the windows, and taken away the altar to set up a simple table in its stead. She went, even though malice whispered all around us and hatred muttered after us like pattering footsteps. She never missed a service, even after she was scratched on the cheek, scored above the breath with a steel pin to break her power as a witch. She did not even flinch, just stood, head bowed, while her blood dripped down, spotting the worn stone flags on the ground.

"Mary? Mary?" I felt a hand shaking me. "Our prayers are ended."

It was Martha. I looked about as if waking from sleep. Even the most devout were stirring and stretching. I went to move too, but my head swam and I staggered a little. Martha's grip on me tightened. I saw the minister's pale eyes narrow. For a moment I was afraid he had seen right into me, guessed my true nature, but then his mouth, thin as a razor slash, twitched with approval. I lowered my eyes. He had taken my rapture for excessive devotion. I could breathe again.

## 10.

*Our prayers are answered.* The mist disappeared, torn apart by a fresh wind blowing steadily from the east. I joined in the thanks, as fervent as the rest. Tarrying here is tedious. I want to be gone.

We left the inn and made our way to the squat tower that marks the West Gate of the city. The ships stood anchored at the quay; beyond them lay the sea. We went through the massive archway in ones and twos and little groups, carrying babies and baggage, carting bundles of bedding and cooking utensils. We picked our way between rubbish and puddles, trying not to drop things, hoping that we had all we needed, parents calling to children not to run off, not to get lost. Each person, caught up in the occupation of the moment, had stepped through with no seeming pause or hesitation, although this is the Gate of No Returning. There will be no coming back.

I had never been on a ship before, nor even seen the sea until a day or so ago. Even then it was through a mist, and all I saw was water lapping oily and thick round the hulls of the ships. To me the vessels looked huge. Our ship, the *Annabel*, seemed to stretch nearly the length of a street. I was staring up at it when Martha tugged at my elbow. The crowd behind us had been pressing forward, impatient to get onboard.

The ship smelled of tar and new wood. As I stepped onto the deck, I felt the subtle rocking motion beneath my feet. I clung to the thick rope held taut and creaking by the masts and spars high above me. I was no longer on solid ground. I looked out, away from the land, to the sea, gray and green as a pigeon's wing. Beyond the harbor, the water looked darker, and white-crested waves marked the endless sea roads where we were bound to go.

When all were aboard and the ship was loaded, we were called to assembly. I stood with the others, head bowed, staring at the wooden planking, scrubbed white and caulked close so no gaps showed in it. Elias Cornwell led us in prayer while the great ship strained at its ropes, as if anxious to be gone. All its human cargo fell silent. The captain ceased shouting and giving out orders. He and his sailors stood bareheaded, solemn as Elders, while the minister asked for God's blessing upon us:

"'They that go down to the sea in ships: and occupy their business in great waters;

"These men see the works of the Lord: and his wonders in the deep.'"

After our prayers were over, we were directed below to the great cabin that was to be our home. It seemed a great expanse at first, running nearly from one end of the ship to the other, but it soon filled up until each person's space was but a bed width.

The sailors sweated and chanted above us, hauling sail and heaving up the great iron chain of the anchor, and we set ourselves up in little groups, piling and positioning our belongings to make enclosures.

"Packed as tight as the cattle in the hold," I remarked as we arranged our bundles.

"And likely to smell as rank." Martha nodded toward the slop buckets in the corner. "Here, strew this in your bedding. I plucked it from my garden just before I left."

She reached in her pack and handed me a bundle of herbs: lavender and rosemary, fresh and pungent, and meadowsweet dried from another season. The scent took me straight to my grandmother's garden and my eyes blurred with tears. Martha went to speak, but her voice was drowned by a fresh flurry of shouting from above us. The heavy mooring rope fell with a dull thud to the side of the ship. Then the movement changed, rising and falling in sudden surges of motion. The mainsail cracked as the wind caught it, and the whole ship veered, causing people to stagger. We were away.

journey two: the voyage

## 11. March 1659

*Good weather and fair winds held.* The sailors praised the pastor until we had passed Land's End, saying that his prayers had worked, but at night I dreamed of blessings of a different kind. All along the coast I saw women in high places, on craggy headlands and jutting promontories, keeping a watch for our passing. Some were standing, long hair streaming, arms outstretched. Some sitting on rocking stones, staring out as if from thrones. I dreamed myself near enough to see their faces. I knew that they had been sent there by my mother. Word had gone out to protect me. I am her daughter and she is a most powerful witch.

## 12.

*Thirty-six paces up,* nine across. That is the main deck. Fourteen paces up, eight across; that is the great cabin where we live. This is my world. I had thought the ship large when I first saw her, but the farther we are out on the ocean the smaller she seems, until now she has shrunk to walnut size, like some little faerie ship surrounded by the deep, green sea.

Captain Reynolds is housed in a little cabin tucked at the blunt end of the ship, under the half deck. The sailors bestow themselves and their belongings where they may. There are few private cabins. There are other passengers besides those of our party, and we are all packed as close as herring in a barrel, though salted fish would smell sweeter—especially when the hatches are closed. The Reverend Elias Cornwell is one of the few to have a cabin to himself. It is a little space, but private—a great luxury compared to the rest of us. He is afflicted by seasickness so badly that daily prayers are led by one of the Elders.

He is not alone. Many others are similarly stricken. Martha is kept busy among them and I help her. Reverend Cornwell has no wife or female relative, so it often falls upon me to tend to his needs. I do not look forward to this. I know something of herbs and healing, but looking after the sick is not a pleasure to me.

The Reverend Cornwell's cabin smells sour—of vomit and the slop bucket. There is a small window with a sliding wooden shutter, which I am quick to open. Under the little window is a writing flap. Normally this is fixed flat to the wall, but once in a while it is down and covered in writing materials. There is a shelf with books upon it and others in a trunk lying open at the foot of the bed. Religious works mostly, Bible commentaries and collected sermons. Some are in English; some are in Latin.

I was examining these to see if there was anything of interest when I heard a voice from the bed. I started up, more in surprise than guilt. Reverend Cornwell rarely acknowledged my presence.

"You can read?"

"Aye, sir. English and some Latin. And write."

"Who taught you?"

"My grandmother, sir."

He heaved himself up in bed the better to look at me. His face was ashen above his nightshirt, his thin hair plastered to his forehead.

"And what was she?"

He looked at me sharply. I kept my face clear, but I could feel the pulse beating in my neck.

"A simple countrywoman, sir."

"And she knew Latin?"

"She was taught by her grandmother before her."

I did not add that she in her turn had been taught by the nuns and that we had many of their books, carried off from their library, saved from King Henry's men.

"What is your name?"

"Mary, sir."

"Bring me some water."

I went over to fill his beaker.

"You know your Bible?"

"Yes, sir. She taught me that as well."

He nodded and then his head fell back on the pillow as if any effort was too much for him.

"You write well? Your hand is fair?"

45

"Yes, sir. Tolerably neat. Why do you ask?"

"I might have need of you. I mean to keep a record of this journey."

"You mean a diary?"

He gave me a look as if he meant nothing so frivolous.

"A journal. A book of wonders, a record of God's remarkable Providences."

"Like the progress we make?" I asked.

The ship was making excellent speed. Many took this as a sign that God's Providence was working already. Even now I could hear the waves hissing against the side. The great sails cracked above us. I braced myself against the lurch and pitch as the ship heaved and yawed with the changing wind. Reverend Cornwell did not answer but closed his eyes and leaned back again, skin tinged green and sheened with sweat.

"I wish to write down, each day, how we fare," he said eventually, "but I am too weak at present even to hold a pen."

"You wish me to write for you?"

He nodded. He could no longer speak. Instead he retched into the bucket by his bed.

## 13

**E**ach day I am called to the Reverend Cornwell's cabin, either to report on any wonders that might have occurred or to scribe for him. There are no wonders, not yet anyway. Daylight and darkness regulate our lives. The days are filled with cooking, tending the sick, minding the children, tidying our portion of the ship. Reverend Elias finds no wonder in that, so I write down his other meditations. These are many and detailed; thoughts buzz about him like flies round a midden. His cabin is filled with a thin sour smell, peculiar to him, and I long to leave but have no choice but to stay and write until my mind aches with the tedium and my fingers are black with ink.

When I do not scribe for Reverend Cornwell, I help Martha. Life onboard is a trial to all. Many of the families are tightly knit by marriage and they occupy different areas of the ship: the Symonds, Pinneys, and Selways fore; the Vanes, Vales, and Garners aft; the Riverses, Deans, and Dennings amidships. Martha knows them all, but I have yet to make much acquaintance with anyone, except for Jonah and Tobias Morse, who occupy the space next to us. People tend to keep to the folk they already know. I have exchanged nods and smiles with Rebekah Rivers, but she seems shy of me, although she talks readily to Martha. Martha treats Sarah, Rebekah's mother, for seasickness. Many still suffer grievously. Martha is very busy.

She is joined in her ministrations by Jonah. He is an apothecary. He and his son, Tobias, are of the Puritan persuasion but not of our party. They joined the ship in London. Jonah is a friendly, lively little man, dark complexioned, with sharp black eyes under bushy gray brows. His hair, what he has of it, is also gray, fringing his bald pate. He is deft and neat in his movements, his hands as small and white as a woman's. He has a cabinet of ingenious design, full of little drawers and cupboards, which hold all manner of things — remedies, bottles of glass and pottery — all packed about to keep them safe. Moved by the plight of those stricken by seasickness, he is offering a concoction of his own making, which he swears will alleviate the symptoms and bring on swift recovery. I told Reverend Cornwell of it, but he has refused all remedies. His affliction is a test sent from God as He tested Job the Prophet. Martha thinks this foolish. She has the skill of healing and recognizes it in others. She thinks Master Morse and his cabinet will be useful to us. Not just on board ship but in America.

Tobias is a very great contrast to his father, being blue eyed and fair complexioned, tall and broad of shoulder. He is about nineteen, a carpenter by trade, just out of his apprenticeship. He is quiet spoken and says little. They share an interest in things mechanical, but there the resemblance between father and son ends.

Jonah has spent much time travelling. He has been as far as Russia, where he was in service to the Czar, and to Italy, where he says he met the great Galileo. He has a great stock of stories to tell. Martha says to take them with a pinch of salt, although I see no reason to disbelieve him. He has a spyglass with which to study the stars and often takes his bedroll on deck and sleeps up there with the sailors. He knows about navigation and the instruments used to calculate our course and is one of the few passengers allowed to approach the captain. He joins him in the quiet starlit watches of the night, and they pace the deck, eyes skyward, Jonah noting differences in the heavens. The new moon appears much smaller from here, and the position of the pole star is much below where it would be if seen in England.

## 14. April 1659

*I have seen my first Great Wonder.*

I was up on deck with Jonah. I spend as much time there as I can. Life belowdecks is becoming impossible. In the confined space, jealousies, rivalries, even hatreds sprout and blossom with strange speed, like plants in a hothouse. Quarrels can break out over anything. I have earned scowls and sneers for I know not what from girls I haven't even met.

Our captain allows us up on deck as long as the weather permits and we do not interfere with the work of the ship. We are lucky, so the sailors say. Some masters keep the passengers battened below for the entire voyage, like slaves out of Africa. I give thanks each time I leave the crowded darkness of the great cabin, with its stench of vomit and slops, rancid cooking, wet wool, and unwashed bodies. I am glad to get out of the din of babies squalling, children crying, voices raised in bickering and quarrelling—all this contending against the constant thud and swish of the waves against the hull.

Jonah and I were watching the porpoises that swim and dive next to the ship. They are not the Great Wonder. They have accompanied us for many days and are no longer anything much to remark about. No, the thing I saw was of the air, not the sea. A huge bird drifting above us in lazy circles on scarcely moving wings, weaving in and out of the sun, seeming to appear and disappear as if by magic. The sailors pointed, open-mouthed, and I stared until my eyes ached. It was a bird of the southern ocean, the sailors said, hardly ever seen in these latitudes at all.

Jonah asked to know more. He is a great collector of information on many different subjects. It had likely been blown off course, they said, probably by some great storm. The sailors are very superstitious, looking for signs in everything. There was much debate among them as to whether this was a good or an ill omen. They were agreed on one thing: When Nathaniel Vale got his fowling piece and took a shot at the great bird, thinking to bring it down for fresh meat, it was as if he had aimed a shot at the captain. The sailors leaped forward and took the weapon from him. They looked up, full of fear. To harm such a bird would bring very bad luck indeed.

The bird appeared untouched, the shot going wide, but it left us, turning in one last wheeling arc and flying away across the trackless wastes of the vast ocean. A feather drifted down, one of the wing feathers: pure white, tipped with black. It caught in the rigging just above my head.

I snatched it before anyone else could. It will make an excellent quill, better than the one I have already, for writing this, my Journal. I have stripped the filaments from the end of the shaft and fashioned a nib.

I have found a quiet place for writing. It is dry, sheltered from wind and spray, used for storing spare ropes and sails and such and little frequented.

## 15.

*The wind that brought the bird* blows strongly from the south, driving us north. Each day the air gets colder. I write wrapped in a blanket now. I can see my breath before my face and my fingers stiffen. The sea is dark green and strangely still, like glass. Huge broken fragments of ice float by us, glinting white and blue in the sun. Some pieces are small, but others are huge, as big as islands. The sailors shake their heads. We are being taken too far north by wind and current. Some mutter about the monstrous bird and view these floating islands with mournful apprehension.

The icy beauty is deceptive. Much of the bulk lies beneath the surface and can rip a hull from under a ship, as sure as solid rock. Jonah Morse has an excellent eye for wonders, and although mindful of the dangers, he is excited. He has seen such before, he tells me, on a sea journey he undertook to the kingdom of Muscovy. I find the ice islands beautiful, particularly in the early morning and in the evening when the ice gleams and takes on color, rose and honey, from the rising or setting sun. They stand up like massive rocks, or the cliffs of some icy wasteland, their bases carved and hollowed with deep blue caves and tunnels.

Our progress has slowed almost to a dead stop. Sailors sound the depth, crying out the fathoms into the cold silence. The captain roams from one side of the deck to the other, pulling at his beard, brow furrowed. Occasionally he raps out orders, relayed by barking shouts and bosun's whistle as the ship slips by the sheer white cliffs rearing straight up from a blue black sea.

16.

*The ice islands are more frequent,* but they are smaller, and it is easier for the ship to nudge a way through them. The weather is cold, however, and getting colder. The deck is slippery and frost forms on the rigging. It is very calm; eerily so. There is not a breath of wind. Ice weighs the sails, which hang drooping from the yards, ready to catch the first hint of a breeze. The passengers mutter, but the captain says there is no reason for alarm, though we are farther north than he would like us to be. Sometimes it seems as if we will be sailing these chilly dark waters forever, roaming the oceans like the great bird we saw, never to touch land again.

## 17. May 1659

*We are nine weeks* out of Southampton. The great bird can live off the sea and its harvest, but we cannot. Food is near to being rationed. We have had little rain, so water is low and grows green in the barrels. There is concern among the passengers, lest when we do reach land the growing season will be over and there will be no time to build houses and shelters before the American winter, which from all accounts can be bitter.

The Reverend Elias Cornwell has recorded all this in his journal. He no longer needs me as scribe, but I still have to report to him every day. He keeps to his cabin, spending his time in prayer and meditation, searching for God's meaning in all the news I bring to him. We have wandered far from our course and have become lost in an icebound wilderness. We must have done wrong, sinned and sinned grievously to earn His displeasure. Either that or there is a witch onboard, a servant of Satan, working some maleficence. He turns, fixing me with those colorless eyes.

"What think you, Mary? Could it not be so?"

I felt my blood chill and bade my heart be still.

"I would have thought"—I measure my words, trying to keep my voice from trembling—"I would think that should the ship founder, the witch would drown with the rest of us."

"*Pah*," he spat, baring his big yellow teeth. "That's what such a one would have you think, but they can float! They can sail in a sieve away from the ship. The Devil looks after his own." He fixed me again with his pale-eyed stare. "And who says *she*? It may be a he. It may be that a warlock sails with us. I will pray that this agent of the Evil One reveals itself. Meanwhile I call a day of fasting and humiliation. We must pray for God's forgiveness."

I curtsied and left him. The fasting will be no hardship. Our meat comes from the barrel green and stinking, the oatmeal is musty and will not thicken, peas stay hard as musket balls no matter how long they soak, and the ship's hardtack is more weevil than biscuit.

## 18.

The fasting and prayer were to be followed by a service on deck. Then a vigil was to be kept until we were delivered from our present trouble. The captain agreed to the first request. The passengers could starve if they wanted to—all the more food for him and his crew—but he would not allow the vigil to take place. He says that a great clutter of people obstructs the work of the ship. His refusal was greeted with a good deal of protest and mutterings of unrest all over the ship, even among his crew. Fears and anxieties that had long been set aside, pushed to the back of the mind, flared up.

All day the disquiet and dissatisfaction spread, as briskly as fire through bone-dry kindling, from mouth to mouth, blowing hither and thither like sparks in the wind. The vigil had grown in importance until suddenly everything depended on it: the success of the voyage, the survival of the vessel, our very lives.

At the appointed time, Elias Cornwell led his flock up on deck. The sailors watched from the rigging or ranged along the rails. The Reverend Cornwell went up to the half deck, which is the captain's domain, and climbed the short ladder to where the captain was standing.

At first the captain would not turn. He stood, a squat and powerful figure, legs planted wide apart, hands clasped behind his back. The younger man approached until he was next to the captain, towering over him. The captain turned, scratching at his thick growth of curly gray beard, squinting up through narrowed eyes, as if taking a reading from the sun. Cornwell, clean-shaven and pale as parchment, looked down at him, preparing to say his piece. He held his hat, turning the brim in his thin white hands, but his manner was more of telling than asking.

The captain's answer did not come immediately. He paced away to the far rail, hands still clasped, one beating into the other. Then he turned, spinning on his heel, and came back. All eyes were on him— Reverend Cornwell's, the passengers', the crew's. The captain looked steadily to each in turn.

It is his ship. His word is law. To give in might be seen as weakness. On the other hand, the captain is a wise man. Agreeing to this would cost him nothing; refusal could cost him everything.

Passengers and crew packed the main deck so tightly that it was hard to move in the waist of the ship. Elias Cornwell looked down at us from the half deck. Beside him stood the Elders, behind him stood the captain with his officers. The captain looked uneasy. He was probably cursing his luck at having a clergyman onboard in the first place.

We stood, hands clasped, heads bowed, and Elias Cornwell's deep preaching voice swept over us, calling on God's Providence, asking for His forgiveness, begging for deliverance, beseeching Him for a sign that we were restored to His purpose. Suddenly the torrent of words faltered. I opened my eyes and looked up cautiously, wondering what the interruption could be. The reverend was standing, head back, chest thrust forward, arms thrown wide. He looked like the etchings I have seen of Christ on the Sea of Galilee.

"We asked for a sign. Now we have that sign. Look, my brethren, look!"

I saw it in his eyes, in the eyes of those standing by his side. I turned and others turned with me.

"The Burning Spears!"

"The Merry Dancers!"

"The Northern Lights!"

Each place names them differently. I had no name for them. Neither had the girl standing next to me. Her eyes grew saucer wide; her hand leaped to her mouth. The sight was new to many others besides. Puritans do not kneel, but many sank to their knees in awestruck wonder. All around me fingers plaited against magic, hands flicked a quick crisscross, mouths muttered prayers to the Virgin. Such strangeness caused many to lapse back to their old beliefs.

Colored lights shone right across the northern sky, leaping and flaring, spreading in rainbow hues from horizon to zenith: blood red to rose pink, saffron yellow to delicate primrose, pale green, aquamarine to darkest indigo. Great veils of color swathed the heavens, rising and falling as light seen through cascading curtains of water. Streamers shot out in great shifting beams as if God had put his thumb across the sun.

"Don't you see? My people, my brethren, don't you see?"

Elias Cornwell was crying, colors shifting and changing across his cheeks, made into mirrors by his tears. Where we were seeing lights, he saw something else entirely. He saw the Celestial City.

"I see it! I see it plain before me!" Somewhere between choking grief and wondering laughter his voice cracked. "'And the building of the wall of it was of jasper: and the city was pure gold, like unto clear glass.' So says St. John the Divine! And so it is! All set about with light, with gates of pearl and shining walls great and high! And the walls are garnished with precious stones, jasper and sapphire, chalcedony, topaz, beryl, and amethyst! And beyond the walls I see shimmering roofs and golden cupolas and glittering spires . . .

"'. . . and there was a rainbow round about the throne, in sight like unto an emerald . . . And before the throne there was a sea of glass like unto crystal . . .'

"I can look no more!"

He cowered back, putting his arm up to shield his eyes as if he really could be blinded. The lights raged, and many folk rushed to the side of the ship, hoping for a glimpse of the vision that held him in its grip. Some cried out that they could see it too, still others stood as if rooted and were taken by a kind of ecstasy, shivering and shaking like Quakers.

The captain viewed all this with growing alarm. A good proportion of his passengers seemed to have been seized by sudden madness and so many rushing to one side threatened to capsize the vessel. He ordered his sailors to their stations and the passengers belowdecks. For a moment it seemed that all were set to ignore him, but the sailors jumped to, and those not moved by the spirit persuaded the others to go below before the captain ordered force to be used.

19.

*All the talk is of what we have seen* and what it could mean. Elias saw the Celestial City, but even for those not blessed with his vision, the lights are a clear omen: of war, of disaster, of plague and pestilence. But for whom?

To Martha the interpretation is obvious. We left a country torn by war from top to bottom, a country where each summer plague threatens one place after another. It is plain enough.

To her.

Not to me.

My grandmother taught me to read auguries, and to me the sign is not so clear. The lights spanned the whole of the sky, from east to west, west to east. Where would the death and destruction fall? On the world we have left, or the one we sail toward?

Jonah Morse has no truck with omens and visions. He has seen the lights many times on his travels. He names them aurora borealis, "lights of the north," and

60

as such, well-known to travellers and seafarers and dwellers in northern countries, as natural a part of the heavens as the sun and the moon and the stars.

He is not slow to tell others his opinion, and they listen politely, but I can tell by their eyes that they do not believe him. He is fast losing any friends he might have made through his potions. They think Master Morse too clever for his own good and do not like being classed as credulous fools.

The talk was set to go on into the night, but all of a sudden, conversation stopped. A wind had sprung up. Above us canvas snapped, cracking like gunshot. Sailors' feet drummed the deck and the air was filled with shouted orders. The ship heeled and turned, and we heard again the steady hiss against the side as the vessel cut through the water. Master Morse lost his audience. Voices rose all around him, giving thanks for this deliverance. Are we not the Chosen Ones? Did not Elias Cornwell see the destination promised? Hands clasped in confirmation. Many believe the wind to be the very breath of God.

### 20.

*Too much wind* is as bad as too little. The wind strengthens until it screams in the rigging, howling like a live thing. It has strengthened beyond any blessing sent by God. We are lifted up by mountainous seas, thrown down into valleys so deep they seem to stretch to the ocean's depths. The *Annabel* lurches and shudders as one huge wave after another thuds against the forward bow, jarring the length of the ship. Icy water cascades through every crack and crevice. Above our heads the sailors' feet race from one side of the deck to the other, their cries and shouts all but lost in the roar of the wind. People huddle together in the fearful darkness, shivering in terror and dread that at any moment we will be overwhelmed and swallowed up. The floor cants at angles that make it impossible to walk, and everything that is not secured is thrown about. We are turned and turned like butter in a churn, at the mercy of the sea, as helpless as a leaf in a mill-race.

The whole world reels and we have no way of knowing how the ship fares or what is going on above-decks. We listen, trying to hear what the sailors are doing, but the hatches are secured and the voices coming down to us are snatched by the screaming wind, thinned to a sequence of cries as meaningless as the call of sea birds. The cabin is filled with the groaning of timber and the crash and boom of water on the hull.

At the height of the storm, a most eerie silence fell about us. Even the children were quiet and the babies ceased wailing. The hush lay unbroken except for a muttered prayer here and there and stifled moans or the sounds of sickness. The cabin was full of listening and waiting for the final rending crash and inundation that would mean the end for us.

Suddenly a scream ripped the silence, tearing it like a cloth. A woman's cry, followed by a sob. Then a space of time, then another groaning cry, and another. A woman in labor. Even the children knew what it was.

Rebekah Rivers came weaving toward us, staggering to find her balance against the ship's jolting movement. She was the girl who first saw me, but I have not had occasion to be much in her company. She is naturally reserved and has been much occupied with helping her mother. Mistress Rivers has suffered cruelly with the seasickness and she is near her time, big with child, so care of the family has fallen on Rebekah. She approached Martha, putting a hand out to her.

"The baby's come untimely, Mistress," she said, her thin hand trembling, her large hazel eyes wide and terrified. "My mother's in need of you. My father asks if you can come quick."

"Of course I can, m'dear. I'll just gather my things." Martha bustled, collecting what she needed, turning to Rebekah when she was ready. "Don't you worry. It will go fine with your mother."

The girl cast a look at the chaos raging round us. Her features are handsome, almost boyish, set in a face that hovers between beauty and ugliness.

"I hope so, Martha." She smiled, tipping the scales to beauty.

"Course it will; never fear. Now, we will need water and clean linen. Go and ask for what they can spare." Martha turned to me. "You can help her."

I followed Rebekah, asking fellow passengers, friends, neighbors, to give us what linen they could. Water is too precious for washing clothes, and nearly every garment had been worn for weeks, but most people had something hoarded to wear fresh for when they left the ship. Their beliefs might be narrow, but in other ways they are generous, openhanded people. They knew the cause and freely parted with shifts, shirts, and underskirts. We soon had more than enough.

"Thank you for your help." Rebekah looked at me over the linen heaped to her chest.

"She's not finished yet." Martha called me to her side. "My hands are not what they were, especially in this cruel cold and damp." She held up fingers reddened and thickened, rheumatic at the joints. "You can help with the birthing."

Rebekah's broad brow creased in a frown as she regarded me.

"You have the skill?"

"My . . . my grandmother taught me." Something about this tall grave girl made me blush and stammer. Her straight look demanded honesty, and even though what I said was no lie, in my mouth it felt so.

"She has the skill, Rebekah. You can trust her."

"I hope so."

I hoped so, too. Her hazel eyes had hardened to agate.

"We will do what we can," Martha said, "but we are all in God's hands."

"And we accept His Will." A man's voice sounded behind me. "In this as in all things. Do we not, Rebekah?"

"Yes, Father," Rebekah replied, but the look in her eyes did not change as she bowed her head. "I will fetch the water."

"My wife is in a bad way, Mistress Everdale." He looked down at Martha. "Do what you can for her." He turned his tall hat in his hand. "Is there anything I can do to assist?"

Martha squinted round. The storm still raged, and although it was daytime, with the hatches shut the cabin was near as dark as night.

"We will need something to light this murk if we are to see what we are doing."

"I'll go fetch candle lanterns."

The light they gave was slight, but we were not allowed oil lamps. They were thought too dangerous down here. Neither could the water be heated, not in a storm like this. On board ship, water was not the only element to strike fear.

He went quickly, relieved to have something to do.

We were near enough in the middle of the cabin, on all sides surrounded by people. Martha looked down at her patient, lying back on a pallet. Sarah Rivers was thin despite the huge bulge of her belly; gray faced, exhausted already, although her labor had only just started.

"Father thought you could do with a bit of privacy."

Tobias came toward us, moving with a sailor's easy rolling gait over the shifting, lurching deck. He had blankets over his shoulder and a pouch of nails and a hammer dangling from his leather belt.

"You best be quick." Martha knelt to Mistress Rivers, who was stirring now, face creasing with the next wave of birth pains.

"Mary, take this." Tobias handed me a blanket as he took out nails.

I reached up but was not tall enough.

"Give it to me." Arms reached round and above me. Rebekah held the blanket as Tobias hammered. She appeared nearly as tall as him.

"Thank you, sir . . ." Rebekah nodded toward him.

"Tobias Morse. Glad to be of service. If I can assist in any other way?"

"You can help her fetch water." Martha looked up from inside the makeshift tent. "Quickly now." She beckoned me to her. "Mary, I need you."

Rebekah returned to her mother's side and stayed, bathing her face, holding her hand, whispering words of comfort and encouragement. It was a difficult birth, a long hard struggle in the fetid half darkness of that little tent. The storm still raged, but we neither heard it or felt it, balancing ourselves to the shifting of the deck as we struggled to birth the child and save the mother. She was very weak, having taken little food for weeks together. The baby could still be healthy, for all her strength would have gone to the child, but he was not in a good position.

"I see him. I see him. Steady. Steady. Steady. That's it. That's it. Good girl. Good girl."

Martha called instructions to me and encouragement to the mother. Together we guided the little body into the world. She cut the cord and gave the child a slap on the rump. There was no response.

"Take the babe," she whispered to me. "I must look to the mother. She's like to bleed to death."

Her arms were slippery to the elbows. She handed the child to me, fresh blood printing his naked form. A boy. Good-sized and perfectly formed. He did not struggle, he did not cry, he just lay solid and lifeless, limp in my arms. Strands of dark hair plastered his head. His skin showed pearl gray through the streaks of his mother's blood. His lips were blue and his eyelids were closed, the veined skin pale violet and parchment thin.

His father took one look and turned away. I looked up from the baby's face into his sister's eyes burning into mine. She held her mother's slack hand gripped in hers. She was about to lose mother, brother, all in one time. I expected to see anguish, sorrow, fear, written there. Instead I saw anger.

I thought what my grandmother would do at such a birth. I opened the baby's mouth, emptied it out, sucked on his nose and spat. Then I breathed gently into him, light puffs of air. I looked again, and although he did not stir or cry out, I thought I saw the skin tingeing pink. I turned toward where Rebekah and Tobias had left the wooden bucket of water, and plunged the child in, splashing the water over him. I heard Rebekah's sharp intake of breath. She was at my side in a stride, as if I were trying to drown the child.

"Have something to wrap him in," I said to her.

The shock of immersion had done its work. His skin was turning from gray to pink. He gave a small cry, little more than the protesting mew of a kitten, but he was alive. I took the rough linen and began rubbing him, chafing the life back into him, then I handed him to his sister.

She wrapped him up and held him tight. She

looked down at his face for a moment and then back at me. Her finger brushed my cheek.

"You are crying."

I looked around as if waking from sleep. Everyone was looking at me. All around was silence. The sailors had ceased shouting, the wind no longer shrilled. The storm was over. Everything was still.

## 21.

*The child is to be called Noah.* Two days after his birth, two small birds came to our ship. One was like to a pigeon, the other like a blackbird, but larger. Both were land birds. It was a sign, sent by the Lord himself, so Reverend Cornwell said. The company gave thanks, and John Rivers decided to name the baby for it.

The wind is brisk, blowing from the northeast. The captain has ordered full sail to be set. The ship keeps an even keel and we make good progress. We expect to sight land daily.

## 22.

*Noah does well,* but his mother is still sickly. He has been put to nurse with another mother who is still feeding her infant. Martha has herbs in her store, which I take to Rebekah. They are to be made into a tea for her mother to help to heal her.

## 23.  May–June 1659

*Yesterday came a shout of "Land, Ho,"* and such a rush up to the deck and over to the side that the ship was like to capsize. A boy, fair hair bright in the sun, came sliding down a rope from where he had been watching aloft. He swung from the rigging and stepped up to the captain, who had already prised a silver coin from the mainmast. The boy took his reward and sent it up spinning, flashing, end over end. He caught it, thrust it into his pocket, and grinned, his teeth white in his brown face.

I crowded with the rest to see the land. It showed as a dark line on the horizon and could have been a band of cloud, but as the ship drew nearer the vision grew into solid hills and rocky cliffs with white waves curling at the base of them.

We are much farther north than we should be, but the sight of land, any land, is welcome after so many days out on the empty ocean. Elias Cornwell stepped forward, thinking to conduct a service of thanksgiving, but the voice of the captain rang out from the half deck.

"I'll thank you to clear the decks. My men have work to do. We are not there yet, parson, and this is the Devil's own coast."

Elias Cornwell opened his mouth to protest, his pale face flushing crimson at being so dismissed and at being called "parson," but the captain turned from him, barking orders for soundings to be made and the skiff to be launched. On board ship the captain rules all. Elias Cornwell led his flock belowdecks. He would conduct the service in the great cabin.

I did not follow them. Calculating that my presence would not be missed, I gazed out to the land. The ragged line of cliffs rose, jagged and stark, spreading in an unbroken line for mile after mile. I shivered. It should have looked welcome to me, but it did not. I reflected on how bleak it is. Bleak and empty.

"Sore sight, ain't it? After so many days at sea."

I turned to find the boy standing next to me, the one who first saw land and earned himself the captain's shilling.

"It looks hostile. Forbidding."

"Aye, it is that. I wouldn't like to have to land just here. This coast is treacherous. Doesn't do to take the ship close in, the rocks here could tear the bottom right out of her." He squinted his eyes toward the shore. "And even if you did land, you'd find nothing but wilderness and meet no one but

71

savages." He turned to me. "You're the girl who saved the babe. They say it was dead and you blew the life back into it."

"I did nothing of the kind," I said, quick to deny any hint of magic. "All I did was clear his mouth and nose so he could breathe."

"I meant no offense. It is just what they say . . ." He shrugged and changed the subject: "You do not go with the others?"

He nodded toward the deck. Voices raised in prayer and thanksgiving rose through the planking.

"No. I prefer it up on deck."

"I don't blame you." He grinned, showing his white teeth. "Stinks down there, don't it? No wonder you like it up here. I've seen you most fine days."

"And I've seen you too. You're the boy who cares for Martha's chickens."

Martha had brought her coop of hens with her, and her cockerel. A woman with hens will want for nothing, that was her thinking, but she had not reckoned on thieving sailors intent on stealing them for the pot. Most had survived so far, thanks to this boy's care of them, but they were kept up on deck, and the recent storm did not treat them kindly. They huddle together in bedraggled bundles, eyes filmed over, stark feathers crusted with salt. They make no sound, not so much as a cluck. If ever creatures craved for land, they do; even the cock has lost his crow.

"That I do." The boy laughed. "If not for me they would all have disappeared down somebody's gullet."

"It would be a brave sailor who took one of Martha's chickens for the pot. She'd wring his neck, like as not.

"I am Mary. Mary Newbury. Martha and I travel together."

"Jack Gill." He held out a hand. "At your service."

I shook the hand he offered. The palm was rough and callused. I turned his hand to find the flesh fissured and split. Saltwater had got into the cuts and cracks, turning them into white sea sores, preventing them from healing.

"I can give you salve for these."

"We all get them. It's no matter." He took his hand away, examining a deep fissure in the web of skin between palm and thumb. He jerked his head toward the voices flowing up from beneath our feet. "Martha is not kin to you?"

I shook my head.

"Nor any of the others?"

I shook my head again and looked up at him, surprised.

"I thought not." He reached for and grasped the ropes above his head. "You keep yourself separate. More often alone than in company."

"They were kind enough to take me in, offer me a place, but . . ."

73

"You are an orphan."

I nodded. I did not count a mother lost almost as soon as she was discovered.

"Me too." He leaned forward in his rigging cradle. "My parents shipped to Virginia. My dad heard there was money to be made in planting tobacco, but he caught a fever and died, my ma alongside him. After that I had to shift for myself."

"You didn't think to go home?"

"Back to England?" He shook his head. "No one would welcome me. I'd be just another mouth to feed. I have no home there, no more'n you have, I'll wager. I got a place as ship's lad and this is home to me now." He gripped the ropes in his hands and leaned out over the water hissing under our bow. "The sea." He grinned suddenly. "The sea's the life for me. I've been up and down this here coast, trading 'baccy and Barbados sugar and rum for furs and salted cod. Then over to England and France, the Wine Islands and Spain. It's a growing trade. There's money to be made."

I looked at him, and he smiled as if reading my mind.

"Even for the likes of me. I make a tidy sum carrying packets and letters. When I've got enough, I'll buy part shares in a cargo—timber, furs, rum, or tobacco. That'll be sold in London and the money used to buy cloth, iron, tools, pots and pans, and other needful things. Sell them and buy again. So it goes round." His eyes shone as he drew a circle in the air, describing the trade. "Then, when I have enough from that, I . . ."

His voice was nearly drowned by a sudden burst of singing surging up from under our feet. They sang a psalm unaccompanied by any instrument, and the sound was ragged, fervent, and loud.

Jack laughed. "Pious lot though, ain't they?" Elias Cornwell's distinctive tenor warbled above the others. "The captain hates a parson worse than a witch." He looked round and dropped his voice as if to share a confidence. "We got one of them onboard."

"How do you know that?"

"Strange things have been happening."

"Like the storm, you mean? But surely there are always storms at sea?"

"I don't mean that, Mary." He shook his head. "I mean other things. After the storm a great light settled on the mast"—he cast a glance to where it stretched up above our heads—"setting it all aglow, like a great candle, but the flame gave no heat." He held out his arm. "Not enough to singe a sleeve. St. Elmo's Fire, they called it, and it is rare to see. Some call it Witch-fire and say that it's her in spirit. And not just that. Some say there's a hare onboard, or a rabbit . . ."

"A rabbit! How could that be?" I laughed. "How did it hop aboard without anyone seeing? Where would it live?"

"'Tis serious! Don't laugh! A rabbit onboard is very bad luck!"

"I don't believe it." I shook my head, still laughing. "It must be the ship's cat."

I'd seen that cat eyeing Martha's chickens, a big evil-looking tabby with a scarred nose and ears all torn and ragged.

"Maybe." Jack was not convinced. "But some say it's a witch in disguise. Some of the lads are Cornish, and they believe there's something here." He frowned. "They know a witch faster than a Witch Pricker. They felt us being overlooked from Plymouth to Land's End, and out beyond the Scillies."

His words sank home. I had not been alone in feeling eyes watching from the shore, but only I knew who they were watching for.

"I've heard no word among the passengers."

I kept my voice merry, seeking to sound light-hearted, although the mere thought of such talk struck dread deep inside me. I'd hoped to avoid suspicion, had not thought that it might follow me even across the ocean.

"Nor will you. Sailors have their own superstitions, different from landsmen. What's strange to us ain't so to you, like a parson onboard or a woman whistling. Ships is odd places. It's not just wind and weather causes upset. Captain'd come down hard on any found spreading rumors. They'd get a lashing.

Besides"——he shrugged——"things is going well at the moment." He grasped the wooden block above his head and gazed out at the fine day; just the right amount of wind in the mainsail to send the ship scudding over the spray. "It's when things ain't, that folk look about for someone to blame for it."

I knew I had not been quite truthful with him. Word had reached the great cabin of strange happenings during the storm, Martha told me, and there had been a ripple of talk about some kind of wild creature onboard. But what Jack said was right. Fears ebb and flow, surging like the waves beneath us. When we were becalmed among the ice, the Reverend Cornwell's mind ran to witchcraft in a trice, and who knows what would have been said had the storm raged for much longer. But now the sun shines and land is in sight. The winds are set fair to bring us safe to harbor. God's eye looks kindly upon us. We bask in His Providence. I am safe. For the moment.

## 24.

*I have the power*; none may doubt it. Whatever I may have hoped, I cannot escape my destiny. What happened today has served to prove that to me.

The day was fine, and I was up on deck, talking to Jack. I do not seek him out (whatever Martha might think), but neither do I avoid his company. His work was slack, and we were conversing about this and that when suddenly there was yelling from up in the rigging. Someone fallen overboard, that's what I thought, for from over the side of the ship came the sound of loud splashing.

Jack took me by the hand, laughing at my alarm. He led me up the sloping deck, bidding me, "Come and see."

At first I could see nothing, just a great turmoil in the water. Then I saw something dark just below the waves. It was so vast, I thought it must be an island. The massive shape seemed to rise toward me, and I could see clusterings of what looked like small white shells on the front edge of it. I remembered what Jack had said about a treacherous coast, and started back from the rail, taking this to be a rock. If we were to hit it, we would surely be lost.

Free from the mass of the sea, water streamed away down the shiny black humped surface, and suddenly there was a strange trumpeting-hissing noise and a mist shot up, so fine that a rainbow shone through it. There was a strong fishy stench, and I saw a great mouth, curved into a permanent leering grin. Then the creature was gone, as quickly and mysteriously as it had appeared. A leviathan. A great fish, like the one in the Bible that swallowed Jonah. It looked big enough to swallow us, ship and all. Another Great Wonder for the book Elias keeps.

"It will not harm us." The great tail paddled the water, and Jack leaned over the side to watch the creature descend into the emerald depths. "There is no need to fear. Look yonder. There are more."

I followed out where he was pointing and, sure enough, great fountains of water spouted up from more of the enormous creatures. Despite their huge bulk, they could leap right out of the water, landing with a great splash and a slap of their powerful curving tails.

"I have never seen such fish."

"They are not fish," he said. "They are whales. Their blood is hot. They do not have gills. They breathe like you and me through the holes in their heads."

"I do not breathe through a hole in my head."

"What is your nose? What is your mouth?"

I laughed. I had not thought of it like that.

"One day I mean to hunt them." He mimed picking up a harpoon and flinging it over the side. "I mean to have my own ship, and I will hire men to go after them, for they are here in abundance and there is great wealth to be made from them . . ."

He leaned on the ship's rail and stared out at the great creatures swimming around us. Maybe it was the sea glittering beneath him, but his eyes seemed full of coins.

The sun was hot above us, and the ship quiet, except for the creak of canvas and the hiss of the sea below. I too stared down at the water, and the shimmering surface seemed to act just like the scrying bowl my grandmother had used to tell the future. People would come to consult her, and she would set up a bowl of clear water. She would stare down into it and visions would come unbidden; some showed the past, some showed what was to come. I had never tried it, although she thought I had the Sight. But now, as I looked, I saw.

Scenes came in a jumble, not ordered by time.

A boy, scarce more than a child. He is standing at the open door of a rough wooden hovel. His face is sad. His fair hair is dirty and unkempt, falling into blue eyes stripped of all merriment. He stays for a moment, uncertain. He glances back into the dark recesses of the hut, then he squares his shoulders and sets out down the dusty red path. He walks head down, looking neither to the left nor the right as he passes through fields full of strange plants with big flopping leaves. The plants grow taller than he and are spaced apart in rows. Although I have never seen them before, I know that they are tobacco. Through the leaves a great river gleams. A small narrow boat is tied to a little dock. It rests like a toy on a tarnished mirror. The boy gets into the craft, casting the rope off, and the river takes the boat, twirling it like a twig drifting on the current.

The image fades and next I see a young man, grown. He is dressed in a dark coat, buttoned to the neck, fur at the collar. He is bareheaded, his cap of bright hair shining in thin winter sunlight. He stands next to another river. The water is gray, slow moving, sluggish, and cold. This river flows through a great city. Buildings tumble down to the shore and crowd the bridge that crosses to the opposite side. He laughs, his white teeth shining, his breath curling in the air. In his hand he holds a purse bulging with gold.

Now I see him older, bearded, wearing a captain's blue jacket. He is standing in the prow of a long narrow boat. Some men are rowing, others crouch forward, pointing like dogs all in the same direction. They hold weapons with barbed points, ropes curling from long wooden shafts. Behind them a ship stands at anchor, sails furled. All around them other boats plough through the choppy sea, hunting the whale.

The waters churn and froth. A huge blunt head breaches, narrow mouth open and armed with teeth. Harpoons dangle like darning needles from the creature's gray side. Baited beyond fury, the great whale turns with a lash of its huge tail and lunges toward its tormentors. It swims with powerful beats, making waves as great as a ship in full sail. Then the sea settles and the crewmen look about, wondering where their quarry has gone. The water begins to seethe around them, like a kettle coming to a rolling boil. The enormous head breaks the surface right underneath them, as if the animal had intelligence, as if it has marked the spot. The whale rises, pushing the boat up and up, out of the water, taking it high into the air, to lie like a broken toy upon its own broad back. Some men tumble headlong into the churning water; others hang, bound to the shining flanks in a tangle of ropes and rigging. Then the creature dives. Whale and boat disappear in a welter of blood-streaked foaming water. Gradually the sea calms. Pieces of wood float on the surface but there is no sign of the men.

"What is it? What is the matter? What ails you? Are you ill?"

I was back in the present and Jack's hand was on my shoulder, callused and scarred but still a boy's hand, brown and supple. I shook my head. "Nothing."

I have seen his past. I have seen his future. I know how death will come to him, and I feel the knowledge like a burden. Grandmother said never to reveal the manner of someone's dying. There is no help and no avoidance. What will be, will be, but to know too soon will color someone's life, darkening the hue for them, stealing the light.

Jack was looking at me, his blue eyes bright and puzzled. I thought he would demand to know more, for

82

he is shrewd and sharp-minded, but just then the captain began shouting, "Hey, you there! Jack! I'm not paying you to idle the time away talking with wenches! Look lively, or you'll feel a rope's end across your back!"

Jack jumped to, leaving me alone, and I was glad, for I had much to think about. The visions came to me unbidden, just as they did to my grandmother, but I knew the gift did not come from her. It comes from my mother. This is art of a different order, beyond my grandmother's power. I felt it settle about my shoulders like a weighty mantle.

## 25.

*Contrary winds hinder our progress* somewhat, but land to starboard keeps all in good spirits. Life onboard has eased. The seas around us teem with fish, and the captain has ordered boats ashore to find fresh water and to forage for whatever food the wilderness affords.

Jonah Morse has made up a salve, and the cuts on Jack's hands are healing well. He has been kept busy about his duties, so I have not had much chance to speak with him, but he knows where I am. He comes to the sail locker, where I hide in the day to write. We meet there and talk, although he risks a whipping if he is caught.

I tell little about myself, but he makes up for that. He talks for both of us. He tells me of the places he has been and what he has seen. I do not know how much of that to believe; sailors are famous for their stories. He also tells me of his plans and dreams. He tells me of Salem, the port where we are bound, and of the handsome houses being built there and the fine wharves for the ships to land their cargo. One day he will build like that, he says, only bigger and finer and in stone, not wood.

"You see if I don't."

I laugh, because I don't doubt him, and that is when we begin pretending: that while he is away sailing the seas and making his fortune, I am at home, waiting for him, and when he comes back he will marry me. He will build a fine house for us and bring me things to fill it: furniture from London, silks and velvets from Paris, tulip bulbs from Amsterdam. I laugh and so does he. We know it to be fantasy, but sometimes I find myself thinking at night as I wait for sleep: making lists in my head, planning the rooms in the house, planting the garden, even thinking of the children we will have.

Then I stop. I have seen Jack's life to come, and I did not see myself in it. Even if we were meant for each other, even if we were destined to be together, I know I would be waiting all my life for the day when he would go to sea and never come back to me. The

Sight is a curse, not a blessing. I wish that I had never seen anything.

"Where do you disappear to?" Martha asked today, as she snipped a strand of thread.

"Just up on deck."

"Not to meet that sailor lad Jack again? Surely the cuts on his hands are healed by now?"

"No," I said, but she knows I am lying.

"The Reverend Cornwell has been asking for you," she said, looking down at her stitching.

"What does he want?"

"You have a fair hand, so he says, and he wants you to scribe for him again. Have a care, Mary," she added, folding the cloth over her worn fingers. "Tongues wag."

"What do I give them to wag about?"

"You are a lone girl, nearing womanhood. You need to have a care how you conduct yourself with that sailor lad—"

"We are friends! Why—"

"Not just him." Martha nipped a length of thread between her teeth before starting another seam. "The Reverend Cornwell."

"What!"

"He's always asking for you."

"I *scribe* for him. Surely—no one could think—" I stopped, appalled, and then began to laugh.

"Hush!" Martha gave me a warning look and glanced about at the crowded cabin. Even the bedding has ears. "Some would think him a good catch, a very good catch for a girl in your position."

"Well, *I* don't!" I could feel my temper rising. "I—I think it's . . . Why—he's, he's . . ." I shuddered and shook my head. "He wouldn't think of me. I am too lowly. You must be mistaken."

"Maybe." Martha shrugged. "I know the way a man looks at a maid. Here," she said, taking lengths of cloth from her workbag and finding needle and thread. "You can get on with this."

"What is it that you are making?"

"Seaming up cloth for a quilt cover." Martha had made a small living as a haberdasher and dressmaker. She had brought what was left of her stock with her. "The winters out there are bitter, so they say, and there is nothing like a quilt for keeping out the cold. These lengths are good for nothing else." She spread the pieces for me to see. Dark wools and linens, in earth browns and blacks, forest greens and indigo. "You can stitch 'em together. You are a good needlewoman, Mary, and it'll keep you out of mischief." She regarded my ink-stained fingers critically. "It is a more fitting occupation for a woman than writing." She shook out the material she had been working. "And the way things are, perhaps we ought to make a start on your marriage chest."

She winked at me then, but I did not wink back. I know she was half joking, but marriage! I had not thought of it beyond a game of pretend. I do not want to think of it in any other way. But Martha is my only protector; it would not do to upset her, so I bow my head and spend my afternoons sewing and snipping like a goodwife.

## 26.

We are nearing the end of our long journey. We have entered a great bay dotted with many small islands. To the west of us lies a line of high hills. Jack points out landmarks on the shore: Mount Desert, the Campden Hills, Agamenticus, Cape Porpoise, Pascataquac. Some are known only by their Indian names, others have been named by sailors. The wind blows from the land with a garden scent of trees and earth and things growing. I gaze at the sea dashing itself against tall cliffs cloaked in dark green forest, and I think the coast looks unknowable. Empty of life.

## 27. Mid-June 1659

Last night we stood off between Cape St. Ann and the Isles of Shoals, waiting for the right wind to take us toward our harbor. We woke to see Marblehead looming up on the western horizon, but then fog came, shrouding everything, slowing our progress in toward Salem. The sailors sounded the depth beneath our hull every few minutes, calling the fathoms back to the captain. The main ship channel passes between two islands, and the approach to the harbor is narrow and hazardous.

The mist cleared after noon, allowing us the first glimpse of human habitation since land had first been sighted. People crowded up on deck to see ships clinging like insects to the wharf. Behind the quay lay the square squat buildings and triangular roofs of Salem.

Deck and cabin are loud with excitement, but I do not share in the general joy. I do not know what this place has in store for me. The ship is familiar to me; it has been home to me. I would rather stay onboard.

I was watching from the ship's bow when Jack swung down from the rigging, light as a cat.

"Here, Mary, this is for you."

It was the coin he had been given for first sighting land. It was broken in two.

"Half for me. Half for you. Keep it to remember me."

"You have come to say goodbye?" This made me more despairing than ever.

"I reckon so. For now anyway." He looked toward the nearing shore. "We will soon be into port and I'll have to look lively."

"But I'll see you in the town!"

He shook his head. "I reckon not. We sail for Boston on the morning tide. That's why I thought to say farewell now. Later, there mayn't be time."

I did not know what to say. I had not thought to part in this way, had not expected it to come so sudden. Jack was like the brother that I had never had, more than that. I turned away in confusion.

"Do not be sad. I'll come back and find you. This"—he held up his half of the coin—"this will be a sign. One day the two halves will be joined. You have my word on it. I'll never forget you, Mary, and I never break my word."

He leaned toward me, as if he would kiss me, but just then a voice roared out.

"You, boy, Jack! Get up to the lookout!"

He looked to leave me but darted back to kiss me anyway. I thought I saw the captain grin, and then Jack was off, up into the rigging. I watched him sitting on the crosstree, as tiny as a child's toy. My mouth burned and my fist closed over the broken shilling. I know that this is the last I will see of him.

the New World

## 28. June 1659

*We came into harbor* on the early evening tide, and it seemed as though the whole town had turned out to greet us. Men, women, and children surged forward, voices raised, yelling out greetings and shouting up for news. Some passengers went below to gather their things, but most stayed up on deck to witness the moment of our going in. They lined the rails, scanning the faces in the crowd below. I felt the mood around me change from elation at our safe arrival to anxiety. They turned to one another with slight shaking of their heads and then looked back to search again. I asked Martha what was the matter.

"There's summat amiss. The brethren who went before us—at least some should be here, and none is."

She left me to join a knot of others. I could not tell what they were saying, but I could hear the rhythms of worry in the rise and fall of their voices.

It took a long time for us and all our goods to be unloaded from the ship. The Elders and the Reverend Cornwell were the first to step ashore. They stood in huddled talk with the leaders of the town, leaving others to supervise our disembarking.

At last we were all on the dock. Then it was the turn of the beasts we brought with us. Gaunt cattle and hogs, sheep and horses, emerged blinking from the confines of the hold. They were hoisted and winched across, legs dangling. A good number had died on the voyage. Those that remain stood, legs wobbling like newborns, bellowing and bleating their bewilderment. Martha's fowl, the few that remained, lay huddled in their coop, as lifeless as bunches of rags.

I wanted to go back onboard. Homesick for the ship, on dry land I felt as bewildered as the lowing beasts. The ground felt strange beneath my feet. The light was glaring, the air hot and still. It was stifling, even there on the quay, and I did not like all the people staring at me. I wanted to go back. I wanted to find Jack. But that was impossible. There could be no going back. The last of our goods had been unloaded, and new cargo was swinging onboard. We ceased belonging to the ship as soon as we set foot onshore.

Family groups gathered in clusters among the barrels, boxes, crates, and sacks. They stood on the quay, their personal things stacked around them, waiting for news. Anxiety grew. No one knew what we were to do.

The Elders had gone with the Salem men. When they returned, their faces were grim. Elias Cornwell climbed up onto a barrel. He stood to address us, arms stretched. A black shape rimmed with light, he cast a long shadow in the setting sun.

First he bid us bow our heads before the Lord and offered a long prayer of thanksgiving for our safe deliverance.

"We crossed the ocean to join our brethren and make a new life in a new world, a pure life, free from outside interference. We are arrived, safe delivered, for which we thank God and His Providence."

These words brought a quick pattering of amens, but then a voice called from the crowd: "What of our brethren? What news of them?"

"Aye," "What news?" "What news?" The questions rustled round the crowd, repeated from mouth to mouth. Elias Cornwell lifted his arms higher to quell the muttering.

"Reverend Johnson and his flock are no longer here." The muttering grew to a roar. Elias Cornwell had to raise his voice to be heard over the din. "Hear me, good people, hear me. The leading men of the town tell me that Pastor Johnson has taken his flock, leading them like Moses, into the wilderness."

The sound from the crowd grew. "What are we to do? What are we to do?"

Reverend Cornwell's voice took on the edge of command. "We must ask for God's guidance until our own way forward is clear. Meanwhile the good people of Salem have opened their houses to us, offering shelter in the spirit of Christ, for which we thank them. Tomorrow there will be a meeting of the Elect in the Town Meeting House. Until then I want each one of you to spend time in prayer and reflection."

He lowered his arms and bowed his head, the signal for a period of silent prayer. We stood, our shadows lengthening in the last rays of sun, the dust beneath our feet taking on a golden cast. We were on solid ground, but I found myself swaying, my body moving still to the remembered rhythm of the ship.

We have arrived, but we are strangers in a strange land. This dust looks the same, settling on my shoes like the dust of home, but it is different. I did not suffer seasickness on the voyage, but now sudden nausea all but overwhelms me.

## 29.

*It is the night* of our first full day here, and the feeling of strangeness continues. Rebekah and I explored the town in the company of Tobias, but none of it seems real to me. It is like being in a dream or the world of Faerie, where all seems familiar until you look carefully.

It is hot, hotter than an English summer, and much more humid. The heat does not fade with the setting of the sun; it seems to increase until I find it hard to breathe. I cannot sleep. That is why I am writing my Journal. I write at the window. The table upon which I write is a shelf cut into a great forest tree that is part of the frame of the house. I take light from the sky. The night is very clear. The moon hangs low and large, like a silver lantern, and the stars blaze across in a great arc. I recognize constellations, but even my untutored eye can see that they have changed. It is as if a great hand has twisted the spheres out of their positions.

On the ground fireflies give out little points of light and crickets and frogs call into the night. The scent of new-worked wood is everywhere. Nothing is old here; little is built of brick or stone. Most of the houses are wood-framed and clad in planks, their steep pitched roofs tiled with wooden shingles. Even the oldest buildings have scarce had time to weather. Few of the buildings are very large or very elegant. Most are small to middling, built for strength and shelter and to keep out the weather.

The people resemble their dwellings in that none are very mean and none of very grand estate. I have seen no beggars, sturdy or otherwise, and no very rich people either. Dress is no marker since all dress the same, in colors sad and sober. Blacks, browns, grays, russets, and greens, unadorned with lace or silk. What they wear and cannot wear are dictated by law. They are strict in this, and I suspect in much else. It is hard not to notice the gaol, the stocks, and the whipping post.

The good folk of Salem show us how life will be. This is no land of milk and honey. Their faces show a history of work and hardship. They have built their life from nothing, fashioned it from the forest. Belongings brought from home are few and stand out among furnishings made from what they find around them. Pewter is for display only. Even the plates and bowls and spoons are made from wood.

The people are hospitable, sharing their houses and food with us, but they are dour. Even the way they speak is different. A marked nasal twang harshens each pronunciation. They give us porridge to eat and meat and vegetables all boiled together. The food is fresh, and each mouthful tastes like manna after weevil-riddled biscuits and salted pork half rotten from the barrel. Most of the food is the same as we would cook at home, except for the porridge, which is bright yellow in color. It is made from the corn that grows tall in the fields and gardens surrounding the settlement. There are other plants too; beans and a low creeping plant with large fruits something like a marrow in taste but that swell round and orange. At least the land seems fertile. One of the first things Martha did was kneel down and scoop up some dirt.

"Good growing earth, that's what this is," she said, crumbling it between her fingers, showing it to Jonah. He nodded his approval, smiling his pleasure. They are going to plant together. Not just crops to eat. They are planning a Physick Garden so that they can grow the herbs they need to make medicine.

Jonah and Tobias are lodging with us, along with Rebekah and her family. We have all found a place at the house of Widow Hesketh. She welcomed us in readily enough and sat us down and fed us, but she is of the unsmiling type, and her hard life shows in her face. She's no beauty, that's for sure, I heard Jonah whisper to Tobias as they went up the stairs, and I'm afraid he's right. She is spare of build, tall and angular, with red raw hands as big as a man's. She lives with her son, Ezra. Together they keep an inn in the town.

Her husband died soon after their arrival. She told us the story of it one evening after dinner when we were all sitting round the fire, soon after our own arrival.

"He's yonder in the burying ground," she said with a jerk of her head. "Along with a good few others. Weren't nothing here when we came, and our ship arrived late in the season, too late for planting."

At those words John Rivers glanced up with a look of unease. We too are late for planting.

"Terrible crossing we had. Held up by storms, sickness onboard. We arrived with precious little food left and many of our party weakened beyond recovery. Winter carried 'em off. The Lord took 'em to Him, including my Isaac." She paused in her telling and looked down at the kerchief twisted in her hands. "We didn't have it as bad as some, but we've had our starving times, that we have. The town's changed since

99

then, mind. No one goes hungry now." She leaned from her settle to stir the fire. "No telling what it's like upcountry. Wilderness land. What you don't take with you, you must do without. Check your provisions, is my advice. Buy more while you can. If you can't plant, you need enough to tide you over until the crops come in next year. Winters are cruel harsh here." She fixed John Rivers with her hooded eyes. "Look to your bairns, your wife. They'll not get through a winter here with empty bellies."

### 30.

*John Rivers has followed* Widow Hesketh's advice and gone with Tobias and Jonah to examine the goods that they brought from England. Anything spoilt on the voyage must be replaced, and anything that we may have forgotten, any extra supplies, must be purchased before we leave the town and go into the wilderness.

Today was a market day and the town was thronged with people, both settlers and those just in from England, all come to buy needful things. Martha stayed to help Widow Hesketh, so Rebekah and I went together. It seemed that everyone from the ship was there. There was an air of merriment about, a feeling of gladness at being safe delivered. Relief at being on dry land again, at having a chance to bathe and rest, to wash dirty ship-worn clothes and shake out the things that had been kept to wear on arrival. We were stopped every yard or so by people enquiring of Rebekah how baby Noah does, and about her mother.

"She does very well, thank you," Rebekah replied in her grave, quiet way. "The baby too."

Few spoke to me. They look in my direction and then quickly away. Even after all the weeks at sea, they still do not accept me as one of the congregation. Not that it matters. Martha, Jonah, and Tobias are all the family I need, and since the birth of Noah, Rebekah and I grow closer, like sisters. When we first met I thought her unfriendly, but I have learned better since then. Her reserve does not come from hostility; it comes from shyness, an awkwardness toward those she does not know well.

She is hardly a chatter-basket, but that is just her way. She only speaks when she has something to say. She is careful of the feelings of others. She does not pry into my past; I do not ask about hers. That is not unique to us. I have a feeling that the same is true of many here. They have crossed an ocean to make a new life and are content to allow the past to dwindle and fade behind them, like the last sight of land.

Not all the traders here were Puritans. There were packmen and peddlers about. Deborah Vane, her sister Hannah, and their friends Elizabeth Denning and

Sarah Garner were busy rummaging through the wares of one such, eager to discover forbidden fripperies, when one of them looked up and saw us.

I knew them by sight from the ship. They spent the first half of the voyage groaning from seasickness. When recovered enough to go up on deck, they spent the rest of the time flirting with the sailors or huddled together talking about sweethearts and weddings, wanting to be goodwives before they have left their girlhood. Today they were dressed in their best, out to impress. Their clothes were still creased from the hold and not properly aired, so that they gave off a faint smell of mildew and mold. Their mothers obviously did not have Martha's way of spreading sweet-smelling lavender between the layers of clothes.

Deborah and Hannah Vane. They are aptly named, at least Deborah is. She is the leader. Near to Rebekah in age, she has a certain plump prettiness, and today her cheeks were pinched to pinkness, her lips bitten to cherry redness. Her collar was livened with a breath of lace at the throat, her dark bodice trimmed and edged with silk. The ornamentation is subtle, carefully judged to fall just short of disapproval. Likewise her rusty red hair contrives to escape the confines of her white cap, spiralling down to frame her face in suspiciously perfect ringlets.

Her sister, Hannah, is younger, and shorter by a head, with sharp, weaselly features. The redness in her hair is diluted to a sandy hue. It escapes her bonnet also, but springs in wiry spirals, like unraveled rope. Her eyes are brown, like her sister's, but dark and shiny, like chips of coal. Any beauty to be had fell to Deborah.

The sisters are always together, Hannah's face perpetually screwed round, looking up in puppy adoration, hanging on every word Deborah says. Elizabeth Denning and Sarah Garner defer to her too. She rules the crew. They are ever in one another's company, giggling and whispering. I do not like them. On ship they gave me black looks for no reason, talking about me behind their hands. Today they ignored me altogether. It was Rebekah they wanted as they beckoned us over, but their interest was not in her mother or her baby brother. They wanted to know about Tobias.

"How does Master Morse?" Deborah asked. She kept her face perfectly straight, but there was a gleam deep in her brown eyes, and her question pitched the others into fits of giggles.

"Older or younger?" Rebekah inquired, although she knew well which one Deborah meant.

"Younger, of course, you goose!" Hannah exclaimed in a fresh explosion of giggles, this time at Rebekah's expense.

Rebekah's jaw tightened. She did not like being taken for a fool by one with less sense than a chicken.

"He does well enough."

"Not with you today?"

"He has other business. With my father."

This brought fresh snorts of laughter.

"His father too. They look to our future—"

"Together?" Deborah inquired with a smile. The other girls could hardly contain themselves. Rebekah fought to seem indifferent, but her pale skin began to color in the face of Deborah's insolence.

She has said nothing to me of the matter, but an understanding is developing between her and Tobias. Nothing as clear as courtship; it is still at the stage of looks and smiles, but of late the two of them have been much together. That has not been lost on Deborah and the others. Deborah's smile thinned, and one glance from her quelled the other girls. The gleam in her brown eyes had hardened. Tobias would make a good husband for anyone. He is handsome and well set, a strong young man and a carpenter, a skill highly prized in a world built of wood. I realized that Rebekah has a rival.

Suddenly Hannah shrieked and started back, clutching Deborah's arm.

"What is it?" Deborah tried to shake off the younger girl, but her grip tightened. "What is the matter?"

"Look! Look yonder!"

Hannah pointed a wavering finger into the crowd. The other girls followed the direction of her stare, their own eyes widening, pupils dilating as if something wild and dangerous had left the forest to stand right in front of them. Others were looking also, many drawing back with a hissing intake of breath.

The crowd fell away on either side as two of the native people came walking through the market. Settlers paid them no mind, as if their presence were an everyday occurrence, but those new off the ships stared in awe and wonder.

"Savages!" Hannah shrieked. "They'll kill us where we stand!"

Deborah squealed like a silly young sow, an animal she resembles not a little, and clapped her hand to her mouth. Elizabeth and Sarah clung to each other, dumbstruck with terror.

"They will not harm you!" Rebekah rapped out, her hazel eyes dark with contempt. "Hush! They'll hear you!"

If they did they showed no sign of it. They were bare chested and bare legged, save for soft skin leggings fringed to the knees. They were not wearing trousers or breeches but short leather aprons hanging fore and aft from a narrow beaded belt; perhaps this was what caused Deborah to squeal. They were shod in soft leather bound with thongs, and each wore a sleeveless open vest made of skins. The boy's was faced by what looked like quills dyed in bright colors, red and blue, and arranged in chevron patterns. Their clothes were scant but practical. They were not sweating in the heat like the Englishmen.

They were tall and well-knit, clean-shaven, handsome men, with striking features. They favored each other enough to be related, although one was much older than the other, perhaps grandfather and grandson. They were dark complexioned, but their skin had no redness to it, despite what white men call their kind. Rather it was the deep brown of well-polished wood, speaking of a life spent out of doors, little encumbered by clothes. Their hair fell long past their shoulders, the young man's shining black with a green blue sheen. He wore it loose and shaved on one side. The old man's hair was graying, with a distinctive wide white streak growing from the side of a deep widow's peak. He wore his hair long also, braided back in a thick plait with feathers and beads worked into it.

As they moved through the crowd, the people around them hushed and fell silent. They walked in a pocket of stillness, and it was difficult not to stare. Jonah has told me about the rarities he has seen. Curiosities, strange and precious things, brought from all over the world for people to look at and marvel over. It was as if an exhibit from Mr. Tradescant's collection displayed in the Ark in Lambeth had suddenly come alive and begun to move among us.

I did not squeal like Deborah or hold on to Rebekah, but like the rest, I could not help staring.

The pair moved with silent grace, and as they passed I caught the clean scent of pine needles and wood smoke, quite different from the rank stench of sour sweat, of bodies too long in unwashed clothes, which clung to my fellows.

The young man stared straight ahead, not looking to right or left. The old man surveyed those on either side, but his gaze was incurious, as if the crowd was made up of inanimate things or creatures beneath his interest. His eyes were set deep, dark as damsons, in a face crisscrossed with lines, heavily creased at nose and mouth. His glance flickered to a halt; suddenly his eyes were alert, piercing and sharp. His gaze held mine for a fraction of time, then shifted on, ranging over the crowd again, distant, indifferent, as if he could see right through them.

### 31.

Rebekah's father is concerned. We have been a week in Salem and nothing is decided. We cannot delay much longer, not if we are to build shelters before winter. It is already too late for planting. He is going to the Meeting House this evening to talk with the other Elders. He means to tell them his thoughts on the matter. If we are to go, it must be now. We could stay here, although most of the good land hereabouts is taken, and Jonah is of the opinion that the towns-people are anxious for us to move on.

Widow Hesketh squinted at Martha. "You're a useful body and I'll own you've been a help to me." She paused. "It's not my business, of course, and I dare say you'll be ruled by kin and conscience, but you have a place with me. The girl too." She nodded in my direction and looked back at Martha. Her hooded eyes were dark and unreadable, like the old Indian's. I felt a message pass between the two women without a word being spoken. "Girl her age can always make herself useful. You say she's a good needlewoman?" Martha nodded. "Town's growing; folk need clothes." Widow Hesketh cackled mirthlessly. "Some's even getting back a taste for finery. No shortage of cloth coming in on the ships. You could make yourself a nice little business."

"It's worth considering, I'll own that." Martha looked down at the pieces she was seaming. "A life already set, as opposed to one to be carved from the wilderness."

I looked at Martha in surprise, she'd never expressed that opinion before.

"But they are my people." Martha snapped the thread with her teeth and started on a piece of darn-ing. "And I look to join kin, by blood and marriage.

We've come this far on the Lord's path together. Now's not the time for me to fall by the wayside."

Widow Hesketh greeted Martha's decision with a slight nod of the head. "May God be with you, then. It will be a long journey, and a hard one." She shivered a little even though the night was hot and the fire was roaring before us. "Not one I'd take, neither."

"Why's that, Mistress Hesketh?" I had moved my stool to the far side of Martha's settle, to get away from the heat of the fire. Now I moved it nearer in.

"There are precious few roads, m'dear, and them that's laid don't advance you far into the forest. It'll be not much more than animal tracks you'll be following, and paths made by savages. The forest is no place for a God-fearing person. They do say . . ."

"Do say what?" I asked.

"That there's spirits in there. In particular a black spirit in the shape of a man. The Indians worship him…" She shivered again, drawing her shawl round her. "Nonsense, no doubt, but there's some swears they have seen it, and folk don't like to get caught in the forest. There's beasts o' course, and savages, but that's not what afears them when the sun goes down. That's not what has them spurring for home fast as a horse can gallop." She leaned forward to stir the pot over the fire. "It'll be a hard journey, and you'll get little help from the folk of Salem."

"Because they're afraid of boggarts?"

She gave her bark of a laugh again. "Not entirely. There's another reason. The Reverend Johnson and his crowd, they left here under a cloud. It weren't because of lack of land; there was plenty and to spare round here then. No." She shook her head. "It weren't because of that."

"Why was it, then?" I asked.

"They were encouraged to depart, so you might say. The Reverend Johnson himself is a very difficult man. Almost as soon as he arrived he began disputing with the other ministers. A good preacher but argumentative, troublesome; stiff-necked and arrogant, that's what they called him, inclined to put his beliefs above all others, and that's not Salem's way. Thought too much of himself, that's what they said, almost to the point of blasphemy."

"How do you mean?"

"There's a sight of difference between preaching the words of the prophets and thinking you are one. He behaved like a prophet new come, and his congregation hailed him. That was too much for the other ministers. They declared his beliefs dangerous, accused him of falling into error and taking his people with him. Repent or go, that's what they said. So he upped and left, taking all his flock off into the wilderness, driving their beasts before them, just like the Israelites."

"Where did they go?"

"He chose paths untrod. Ways unknown. Trusting that God would guide 'em where they wanted to go."

"But they settled somewhere, surely?"

"They founded a settlement deep in the wilderness, and we've scarce heard from them since. They rarely come here. Now you arrive, bent on joining them." She turned troubled eyes to Martha. "Truly, mistress, I caution you against it."

## 32.

*We are all called* to the Meeting House. The whole congregation and anyone who might have a mind to join them, like myself, Jonah, and Tobias. We will be asked to choose whether we wish to stay or go. Martha will go, the Riverses too, but I'm not sure about Jonah and Tobias. Jonah likes it here. He wanders the town and the docks, exchanging gossip with townspeople and sailors, swapping news, and gleaning information. He is even doing a little business, selling his pills and potions. I have heard him speak his doubts to his son.

"What do you know of farming? Or I, for that matter? You a carpenter, me an apothecary. We could make a good living right here in Salem. Or try our luck in another town—Boston, maybe. I've heard it thrives—"

"They are good people."

"Good people? Aye. With the zeal of the Lord in their eyes. And what of these others they go to join? We know nothing of them. We are strangers. They may not welcome us. Would it be wise to join them? What do you say? Do we go? Or should we stay?"

Tobias did not reply. He just stretched his long legs before him and drank his ale.

### 33.

*Two men stood at the door* as tellers: Deborah's father, Jeremiah Vane, and her uncle Samuel Denning. We filed in and took our places, strictly according to rank. Elias Cornwell stared down from the pulpit. There was to be no discussion. The Reverend Cornwell did not even sermonize, he merely bid us bow our heads, instructing each to pray in silence, to humble ourselves before the Lord and ask for His guidance. The time had come to decide: to stay here, to go elsewhere and join one of the other towns springing up, or to follow Reverend Johnson's lead into the wilderness. The Elders had already decided. They were all in a row at the front, John Rivers among them.

One by one, the head of each family moved from his place to join them. Then Sarah, Rebekah's mother, moved to her husband's side, leading her children by the hand, Rebekah following, carrying baby Noah in her arms. Although I share some of Jonah's doubts, when Martha went, I went with her.

The families ranged round the sides of the room, leaving just the outsiders sitting down. Jonah bowed his head deeper, whispering to Tobias out of the side of his mouth. The son shook his head, as if to rid himself from flies, straightened his shoulders, and stepped forward to join the others, taking his father with him. Rebekah watched Tobias walk to his place. Across the room Hannah leered up at her sister, and Deborah scowled. I looked over at them and smiled. Where she goes, he will follow.

34.

*Tonight, after supper,* Widow Hesketh bid me sit with her.

"I got a bit of mending wants doing. Let's see what kind of needlewoman you are."

She sat in her usual place by the fire, with me on a stool next to her and a bag full of stockings to darn and shirts to patch. She inspected my work, looking for strength and smallness of stitch. Once satisfied she bid me carry on while she stared into the fire.

"You are welcome to stay along a' me," she said after a time. "There's a place here for a girl that's prepared to make herself useful."

I looked up in surprise, a little taken aback. I did not answer straightaway but carried on with my work, concentrating on keeping the stitches neat and regular. Then I thanked her politely and declined her offer. I might share some of Jonah's fears about what lies ahead, but to stay would mean becoming little more than a servant, and I did not relish that prospect.

"Think on it." Her hooded eyes sought the fire's depths. "I know a little of your history from Martha, and I can guess the rest. You might be safer here. I think you guess my meaning."

"How do you know?" I asked quietly, looking round warily. We were by ourselves in the big firelit room, no other soul even close, but to speak of such things could put us both in danger. If she saw the witch in me, perhaps others could see it. Fear filled my throat and stirred the hairs on the back of my neck. "Is it so clear?"

"Kind knows kind. Whether 'tis a gift or a curse, I can't tell, but I know 'tis not of our choosing." She still did not look at me, but I knew from her words that she practiced the craft. "I was warned of your coming."

"By whom? How?"

"Not for you to know." Her eyes were on me now, and in each of their black centers a twin fire burned.

"But you need to take care wherever you go. Especially here."

"Here? Why here? I thought all were free to start a new life. I thought—"

She gave her cackling laugh. "Bless you, my dear. It is worse here! Folk bring their superstitions with them over the ocean. Once here they find themselves surrounded by the forest. No man can say how far it stretches, infested with natives and who knows what. Faith is like a faint spark in a vast darkness. Their fears grow like bindweed, choking everything."

"I can be careful. I can look after myself."

She cackled again. "That I doubt. But I do not speak just of you." She leaned forward to swing the kettle over the ashy logs. "Martha's a good woman and she's shown you kindness."

I didn't deny it.

"Then have a care, my smart young maid. You're as sharp as a thorn, with a mind of your own. You must keep a curb on your tongue or you'll have more than yourself in trouble. Keep your counsel and look to your back."

## 35

*Our departure has been delayed* yet again. Days drift by and still nothing is decided. The Salem men say we must use native guides, but Reverend Cornwell and the Elders will not hear of it. They argue that they are heathen, the sons of Satan, that we must trust in God to guide us through the wilderness, just as Moses did his people. Not everyone is of the same opinion, even among the Elders. John Rivers came back from the last meeting severely out of temper, muttering that Elias Cornwell can quote all he wants about Moses. The children of Israel were forty years in the wilderness, which is a long while to be wandering and homeless. God took His time before getting them out.

The Salem men will not go without the natives. They say that we are going into parts little travelled, and without native knowledge we are sure to get lost. John Rivers says that we cannot go without help from Salem, whatever the Elders may think. We do not have enough carts or beasts to carry all our goods and people. The Salem men are practical and shrewd. They will not lend us wagons, oxen, and horses lest they do not get them back again.

After a deal of arguing, Rivers and his party have won. We are to have native guides after all. Now there is fresh grumbling. Hire of wagons and oxen will cost us dear, and no one in town will part with a horse.

They are reckoned too valuable to be risked in such an enterprise as this. Now that we are to leave, anxiety and excitement grip the company in about equal parts. Some, it is true, follow Elias Cornwell and put their trust wholly in God's guidance and themselves under His direction. But for most, prayer and contemplation have given way to a fever of anticipation. Some lose themselves in preparation, packing and repacking, checking and rechecking that all is in order, that items needful for the journey have been kept out and the rest stowed and safely loaded. For we are bound for wilderness parts, as Widow Hesketh has warned us. How long it will take and how hard the journey, nobody knows.

I share in the excitement, but I have my own fears. Widow Hesketh's words to me still whisper in my ear. But I cannot go back, and I cannot stay here. Martha has made her choice, and I with her. She cares for me and wants me to travel with her. I know what it is to be truly alone in the world and do not want to feel that way again. Besides, I would miss more than Martha. Rebekah and Sarah, Jonah and Tobias have gathered about me, almost like a family. So I pack and unpack under Martha's direction. If it is my destiny to stay with these people, then let it be so.

journey three: wilderness

## 36. July 1659

*At last we left Salem,* on a brilliant July day, rising to an early morning as fresh and clear as any in England. I remembered my grandmother's garden, sweet with the scent of gillyflowers and roses. I saw again the hollyhocks, delphiniums, and Canterbury bells, shining bright, like jewels in the sunlight. Sadness caught my throat as I thought of the cottage behind, all dark and deserted, the little plot choked and filled with weeds.

We assembled to parade through the town, some riding, some walking, others mounted on carts piled high with goods and belongings. The town turned out to watch us, and it was like a fair, a festival, such as they had at Lammas or Harvest, when processions would pass through every town and village. I was too young to remember, but my grandmother had told me about them. It made me sad that I had missed those times when work could be put off until the morrow and everyone could be gay and merry, at least for one day.

We left the town, and the country spread out before us, green under a cloudless sky. The road forward was broad and well-made, winding off into the distance through land as open as park land and set with tall trees, some standing alone, others grouped in clumps: beech, ash, oak.

I was not alone in my thoughts of home. I saw fleeting joy pass over many faces, each time followed by the same shadowing sadness—as if a dear one long-departed had been glimpsed in the face of a stranger, the long sought but never to be seen again beloved.

We advanced slowly, for we were a large group and truly must have resembled the tribes of Israel in their flight out of Egypt—driving our cattle, sheep, and goats in front of us, rambling along rag and tag, ambling behind the rumbling carts, and spreading onto the sward beside the road.

We were not pursued by Pharaoh's army. We even had time to stop and pick strawberries. They grew in abundance, the fruits large, as big as plums, lush and juicy. We filled our aprons and ate them until our mouths were stained red, our hands sticky.

It began that way, like a high day, a holy day, until even the doubters among us were laughing. Martha rode up on the cart with her chickens squawking. They are all glossy-feathered now, restored to plumpness by corn and scraps from Widow Hesketh. Jonah drove the oxen, leaning back to joke and tease Martha. I walked alongside with Rebekah and Tobias, he carrying one of her small brothers on his shoulders while the others scampered around, glad to be free of the confines of the town.

All day we travelled in this way, stopping only at noon for refreshment, eating the food we brought with us, sitting on blankets, while the animals cropped the grass. We went until sunset, when it was time to set up camp. Elias Cornwell led a solemn service of thanksgiving (I do not know why, we had not even reached the forest), and we built fires and cooked on them like a beggar band. Some slept under canvas shelters, others under the wagons or out in the open, for the night is mild. I write by the light of the stars.

37.

*Roads are few here.* Most long journeys are taken by sea or by river, but we have elected to travel overland.

When we began the day's journey today, the way was still open, allowing us to pass with relative ease, but thick swaths of green smudged each horizon. For a long time the green stayed a blur, getting no nearer. Then the single trees dotting the landscape grew more numerous and clustered closer together; the stands of beech, oak, and pine became more substantial. But nothing could prepare us for the forest itself. As the broad road we took out of Salem diminished to a track, our progress, slow at the best of times, slowed still further. On all sides the great forest loomed. We could only travel as fast as the heavy carts and the lumbering cattle would allow.

The trees massed in a ragged line. The track we were on wove into it and soon became lost in the shadowy depths where towering giants cut the bright day to half-light. Cedars spread huge branches. Pines reared up so tall that their tops seemed to bend together. Rough-barked trunks grew to such girth that four men with linked arms could not reach around them. The leaves and litter of centuries lay thick on the forest floor.

Through the trees we could see only blackness. The cavalcade stopped. Even the animals were reluctant to enter; they turned, lowing plaintively, and the horses stamped and whinnied, tossing their heads. The children no longer played and ran about. They returned to their mothers, clutching at their skirts. Women turned to their menfolk, who stared as round-eyed as their children. This was the Wild Wood, greater than any that we had heard of in fireside stories. To enter was to step into a realm of mystery, and who knew what forces held sway in its dark depths?

Two men stole from the margins, as quiet as ghosts. Truly they seemed like some kind of apparition, for they appeared in the blink of an eye; the space they occupied, empty one minute, was filled the next. They stood before us and uttered no word of greeting. These were natives, Red Indians, the first that many of the company had ever seen. Their sudden presence caused cries of alarm. Some of the women started up shrieking, and some of our men reached for their weapons; the Salem men had to intervene. They were not come to attack us. They stood out in plain sight, bows slung across their backs. These were our guides. They had been with us all along, we just had not seen them. They had come out now because they were needed. Without them we would never find the settlement for which we were heading. Without them we might never be seen again.

Our guides are to be the pair I had seen in the market. The boy and his grandfather were known to the Salem men, and the younger man stepped forward to speak to them. Our Elders gathered too, and all stood in consultation. To the surprise of many, the boy spoke English as well as any in the company. His grandfather took no part in these negotiations; he stood still and easy, ignoring the stares of the curious. Occasionally his dark eyes flicked over us, as if to satisfy his own curiosity. Again I felt his eyes seek mine and hold them, just for a second. Again I experienced that feeling of strangeness, as if he was looking into me. He held me as a stoat might hold a rabbit, then his gaze moved on, and the feeling of strangeness had gone.

By the time they had finished talking, the sun was sinking behind the forest. It was too late to venture in. We had to camp for the night.

The Indians have repaired I know not where. I write by the flickering firelight. Out of its circle all is blackness.

Elias Cornwell led prayers before supper. He took his text from the gospel according to Matthew: "'Wide is the gate, and broad is the way, that leadeth to destruction, and many there be that go in thereat.

"'Because strait is the gate, and narrow is the way, which leadeth unto life, and few there be that find it . . .'"

### 38.

*We have entered the forest proper.* Sometimes the way is as wide as a king's riding; other times it disappears completely, stopped by impenetrable thicket. Saplings and briars have to be cleared, sometimes whole trees, to allow the wagons through. The wagons halt, and Tobias and some of the other men go forward, shouldering axes, ready to cut our way. The woods ring with the sound of metal on wood. Progress slows almost to nothing. It is hot under the canopy of leaves, with hardly a breath of wind, and the many biting insects are proving bothersome.

## 39.

*I have lost count of the days* spent like this. We have food in plenty, and there is more to be gathered in the forest, but the Indians have proved their worth. If it were not for them, we would have died of thirst. The woods, so thick and lush, are as a desert to us, but these men know the site of every hidden stream and spring in the country. They also lead the men to hunt game, adding venison and turkey to our diet. They bring other things too: nuts, fruits, and salad herbs.

We journey each day until the light begins to fade. The overarching canopy hides the sun during the day, but the trunks are bare below a certain level. When the sun dips to the horizon, it shows through in thin fingers of yellow, orange, reddish light. Shadows spread and lengthen. It is a sign that we must make haste to camp for the night. When the last light goes, the darkness is absolute. Down here there is no moon or stars.

Fear grows as the night falls fast upon us. Fear of the unknown. Fear of the darkness.

It is enough to rock the strongest faith. Elias Cornwell prays for protection, to keep us from harm.

"'Yea, though I walk through the valley of the shadow . . .'"

And even his voice shakes.

We are truly in the wilderness. Screeching and howling rend the night. The cries are of creatures unknown to us, not heard in England since ages past. The men take turns to stand guard, muskets at the ready, for such threats are real enough. These woods are home to wolf, bear, and lion.

The forest is also the realm of Satan, and against him and his forces guns offer no protection. "Only prayer is proof against them," Elias Cornwell reminds us, but despite his ministrations, stories of all kinds gain credence and grow in circulation—stories heard in Salem, of a black man and forest spirits; and stories brought from home, of elves and goblins, of all manner of evil things lurking outside the firelight's protective circle.

We camp in a tight ring, backs to the forest, faces to the fire. The Indians camp always a little way off from us. Their small fire shows, tiny as a spark, in the great blackness. They are at home in the forest. If they feel threats about them, they do not show it. They make their shelter seemingly out of nothing, bending young saplings over to make a frame, roofing this with foliage, making beds from ferns and dried leaves from the forest floor. In the morning, when they break camp, they leave no sign that they have ever been there.

## 40.

*I was brought up deep in the woods* and I do not fear the forest as the others do. Grandmother may have been speaking in jest and teasing when she named the Erl King as my father, but as a child, I believed her. He is the Lord of the Greenwood, and I grew up fearing nothing in his domain. Neither do I feel any terror here, even though these woods are mightier by far than any we have at home and as mighty, Jonah says, as any he has seen on his many long journeys in Russia and Bohemia. The forest holds no terror for him either. He finds it interesting. He points out new plants that grow on the forest floor, plants that he has never seen before. At night he slips to the Indian camp to ask what names they call them, what use they make of them. Jonah spends long hours with them, then he comes back and writes their answers in his book, adding little sketches of the clothes they wear, the shelters they make.

Many of our travelling companions think the Indians all to be the same, all savages, but Jonah explains that the native people in New England are divided into nations. They use the same sort of speech and language, only differing in certain expressions, just as is true in different parts of England. Our two guides are Pennacook, and their tribe lives to the north of here. The boy was educated by white people, that is why his English is good. His grandfather speaks little of our language, but he is the one who names the plants and describes their properties. The boy translates for him.

Some nights even Jonah is too tired to do anything but sleep. The journey is difficult. Every day there are new problems: rivers to ford, boggy and marshy ground to traverse, hills to climb, or ways to be cut. More and more are footsore or too weak to walk anymore, but riding on the carts puts more strain on the horses and oxen, so this is the privilege of very few. Nevertheless, we press on, yard by yard, cutting a way through the wilderness with a determination that even the Indians admire. They have said as much to Jonah.

### 41.

Last night, just as evening was coming on, we reached a clearing, a high point in the forest, a good place to camp for the night. From it the trees spread out in all directions, vast as the ocean we crossed to come here. As we looked out, the clouds parted and a finger of light broke from the west. The last rays of the dying sun shone red and golden, touching on a hill some way distant.

"Look! Look there!" A cry rang out, then another. All ran to see what the shouting was about.

Smoke was rising, thin wisps curling up into the sky. The first signs we had seen of human habitation. A few thought it might be a native settlement, but the Indians shook their heads.

"White man's fire," the younger one said, and turned away to stare in the opposite direction. "It is called Beulah. It is the place you seek."

Voices cried out in praise to the Lord and many wept, clutching on to each other. Some sank to their knees, fingers steepled. Although such customs in prayer are frowned upon, old habits die hard. Elias Cornwell did not scold as he would at other times. He led the rejoicing, face rapt, tears streaming.

"We have reached our deliverance. Before us stands the City on the Hill. Beulah, Bride of God."

42.

*The hill is farther* than it appeared. First sighting made it seem near enough to reach out and touch, but the strangeness of the light, joined with hope and expectation, shortened the distance. Another line of hills lies between us and Beulah. There will be many more miles of difficult travelling before we can reach our destination.

## 43.

As soon as we left the hilltop, our goal disappeared altogether, swallowed in the endless expanse of trees. But just as I feared that the vision might have been only that—an illusion—the trees began to thin. The way was wider here, the edges showed signs of having been cut back. The surface had been levelled, the worst holes filled. Fresh hoof prints showed, but they belonged to our riders sent ahead to warn of our coming. Other than these, there were no tracks. Grass and weeds grew freely upon it; the road seemed little used.

All around, the trees were dead or dying. The effect was odd: Why would all the trees die at once? Jonah pointed to rings round the trees, where thick bands of bark had been cut from the trunks. Cutting them in this way causes the trees to die, making them easier to fell. A trick learned from the Indians, to clear the ground for planting. We were nearing the settlement.

We journeyed on without the little sounds that have accompanied us for so long: sudden bird calls, the rustling of animals. Silence filled these woods. Only the drilling of woodpeckers echoed through the creaking trunks. The effect was eerie and not a little sinister, as if we travelled a road used only by ghosts.

The hill stood before us, a river snaking round the base of it. The settlement spread down from the summit, small houses dotting the hillside, smoke curling up from the chimneys. All around, the forest had been cut down and the land cultivated into fields. Men and women were bent upon their business: a man on a roof hammering in shingles, a woman pegging out washing, others weeding and hoeing, walking the rows, checking how the tall corn grows. The light was golden upon them, and they had not noticed us. For a moment we stayed as watchers, as if after all these weeks of journeying, something was holding us back.

Then someone looked up and called out. The cry went up, taken from one person to another. Figures racing up the hillside to take the news met those coming down. Our column broke ranks. Babies and children were swept up, and everyone was running, young and old, weary legs finding new strength. They met between town and forest; old friends, neighbors, relations falling upon each other to weep and praise God together.

Martha gathered her skirts and ran on with the others, to search for her kin, but I stayed with Tobias and Jonah. We stood back and kept to watching. There was no one to greet us, no one to meet us. The Indian boy and his grandfather also hung back. They were looking toward the township, when the old man muttered something in his own language. It sounded like a prayer but could have been a curse. I had no way of knowing. He nodded once to Jonah, and then they turned, stealing off into the forest as quietly as they had come.

settlement

*Not all is joy,* not all rejoicing. Martha found one sister in the burying ground and the other much changed. Little Annie has become Mistress Anne Francis, married to Ezekiel Francis, one of the chief selectmen. At home, according to Martha, Ezekiel Francis was not much above a hired man, but here he owns a great deal of land. He is one of the chief men of the town, and it is clear that Mistress Anne looks forward to her sister acting as servant, with me thrown in as a makeweight.

"I did not cross the ocean for that. You neither. I thought all were free here," Martha told me.

Jonah said we can go in with him and Tobias. Martha can keep house, but she will get equal shares, which sounds fair. Neither of us wants to end up as a servant. Martha's sister is not best pleased, but there is nothing she can do about it.

Others too find disappointment. John Rivers hoped to find his brothers here, only to be told that they have moved on. When he asked where, the townsmen did not know. When he asked why, they just shrugged their shoulders and told him: "This is not the place for everyone."

Sarah found kin here—her sister and brother-in-law are high placed in the town—but it seemed for a time that the Riverses might move on. In the end they decided to stay. Sarah argued that they cannot wander the Colony forever, searching for John's brothers. She is weary of travelling, the children need a home building. They will not want for land here; there is plenty for those who are willing to work it. Rebekah tells me her father is still not entirely happy. He is a deep-thinking man who likes to have answers. His brothers knew he was coming. It bothers him that they should have left without waiting, without leaving word. But it is late in the season, and where they have gone, there is no way of knowing. His wife and Rebekah persuade him to stay.

I am glad of it. Rebekah is the only true friend I have ever had, and I would miss her. Tobias says little, but I know that he would miss her too.

## 45.  September 1659

*The Vanes and others* have families to help them build for the winter. The Vanes live in a compound that is a near village of its own, ruled over by Jethro Vane, an important townsman and leader of the clan. He is a greedy man and quarrelsome. He has already disputed some of the land given to us. His title appears on no map, so his claim cannot be upheld, but that does not stop him complaining. He owns a great many evil-tempered hogs who wander where they will. I think he sets them loose deliberately, for they trample ground that Martha has set aside for a garden. Tobias has promised to build a fence to keep them out, but until then it is one of my jobs to drive them off.

Having no kin to help us, we must shift for ourselves, and there is much work to be done. We have little time to build houses. Two months, three at the most, before winter comes. The land allotted is generous, but some has to be cleared from the forest, and the rest has to be broken and ploughed.

There is much to do, but no one can work on Sunday. The Sabbath is strictly kept. "Six days shalt thou labor, and do all thy work: But the seventh day is the Sabbath of the Lord thy God: In it thou shalt not do any work."

Therefore on Sundays no work can be done, no fires lit, no cooking; even the animals must forage for themselves. Much of the day is spent in the Meeting House on top of the hill. All roads lead to it like the spokes of a wheel. It is the most impressive building in the town. Square built, facing south, with a four-sided roof and a central turret. It is set on a platform of stone slabs, massive and timeworn. They hold the building off the ground. Stone steps wedged one on top of another lead up to the doors.

The walls are rough unpainted clapboard; the bounty heads of wolves are nailed to one side of it. They are nailed in an irregular row, their blood staining the wood with beards of rust and crimson. They are there to remind us of the dangers that lurk in the forest, and to show the wolves who's master here. For some reason, they fascinate me. I've never seen a wolf, alive or dead. These are very dead. Some are rotted to matted lumps, weathered and maggot-eaten beyond recognition. Others are fresh and still retain some of their awesome fierceness. The fur is dry, and death has dulled the staring eyes to opaque blue, but the bloody teeth still snarl defiance.

"I got that 'un." An old man pointed proudly when he saw me looking, then he pointed to himself. "Old Tom Carter. Trapped 'un good and proper."

I know him. He lives hard by the forest. He's nigh toothless and smells of stale liquor among much else. I thought his hut a haystack when I first saw it. It is not much more than a hovel made of mud and thatch.

"You a new 'un?"

I nodded.

"Ain't I seen you in the forest?"

I nodded again. I had ventured in a few times, just to explore.

"You keep a sharp look out then, my maid." He nodded toward the wolf's head. "Don't look much bigger'n a dog, do it? Don't let that fool you. What they lack in size, they make up in savagery. Run you down and rip the throat right out of you 'fore you can make a sound."

The door of the Meeting House is covered with notices: some new, fresh written; others old, the paper yellowed, the writing scarce readable. Wedding banns, orders, and prohibitions, of which there are many.

Thou shalt not . . .

The town is run in strict accordance with God's laws. Anyone disobeying them can find themselves in the stocks or whipped or having to find another place to live.

Sunday service is attended by all; there are no exceptions. The penalty for nonattendance is expulsion. Not just from the church but from the whole community. The sermons go on for hours. Now that Elias Cornwell has come to play Aaron to Reverend Johnson's Moses, they often preach one after another. We sit in rows on wooden benches, women and children one side, men the other. We have to sit ramrod straight. Anyone slumping, anyone nodding, earns a jab in the back from a tithing man, or a sharp rap across the head.

The Reverend Johnson is hailed as a prophet. The people who came here with him almost worship him. They hang on every word he says. His word is God's word and God's word is law. They often write down his sermons to read back later. I sit, head bent, scribbling away, but I write with a different purpose. The pulpit is painted with a great eye. God watches us all the time. I keep my Journal under His gaze.

The Reverend Johnson does look somewhat like a prophet in that he wears his hair long and has a great beard jutting out. Other than that, he looks more like a blacksmith than a preacher, as he is square built, deep-chested, and thickset. The hand he bangs down on the edge of the pulpit is thick as a ham and hairy as a hog's back.

I do not like him. I do not like his eyes. They are very dark, showing like holes between his tangled brows and the line of his beard, as cold and empty as musket barrels. I try to avoid them when they look in my direction. I do not want to be noticed by him.

I sit next to Martha. As newcomers we are positioned on the right, at the back, by the big double doors. This will be drafty in winter, but this place suits me. It is as near as I want to be.

Reverend Johnson's wife and children take the first row.

Goodwife Johnson is as thin as her husband is burly. She stands, easing her back with one hand, her face so pale as to be almost gray. Her mouth is pinched as if she is sucking lemons or fighting back nausea. Martha whispers that she might be with child and hopes not with the same breath. The children sitting in a row next to her must number ten, ranging from a girl of fourteen or so to little ones hardly toddling.

"Not with that great brood she's got already. And there's a raft more buried in the graveyard, poor little mites."

Martha's whisper is hardly above a murmur, but one of the tithing men frowns in our direction. Martha's sister sits in the next row from the front, along with the wives of the other selectmen. She's very proud of this, turning to smirk as we come in.

The Riverses—Sarah and Rebekah and the children—sit in front of us. John sits on the opposite side and near the front. Although too new to have a voice here, John Rivers is an Elder in his own church and is very much respected.

Elias Cornwell is stepping down from the pulpit. The Reverend Johnson is mounting to speak.

"'Remember this day, in which ye came out of Egypt...'

"*We* are God's chosen people, just like the Israelites. Did we not suffer in the wilderness? Was our path not guided? Did we not see a beam shining down like the finger of God? Pointing out this place to us?

"We found a hill already levelled upon which we could build our city. We came upon it famished and were fed. We did no more than scratch the ground and good things were given in *abundance* so that we lived all winter and wanted not. We found meadows here, fair pastures, and sweet water that man and beast may prosper.

"All signs of God's Providence, of His care for us. We called this place Beulah, Bride of God. We wait for His coming, and, I tell you, it will not be long. For Satan has come into his kingdom. He reigns everywhere. His forces are all around us, even here in New England." He turns his shaggy head and bends his black brows on us, the newcomers. "We welcome you, our brethren, and rejoice that you come to us safe delivered, but if you thought to leave the Devil at home, then you would be wrong. If we hope for salvation, we must be ever vigilant. Know you not that the evil one is immensely strong and cunning? Know you not that the Indians are in league with him, worshipping him in their forest? His forces lurk all about, waiting in ambush in fern and thicket. They are even here among us, slithering like snakes, sly and unseen, hiding in the wainscot, like low creeping things . . ."

At last we file out, back to our half-built house. We can do no work, but I see Tobias itching for adze and saw. John Rivers, too. Jonah would rather be working in his garden, but since he cannot do that either, they stand together, hands in breeches pockets, looking at the half-built structure and the half-dug plot.

We build our houses together, side by side. As newcomers we are given plots out from the center, near the forest edge. Our nearest neighbor is that old man Tom Carter. His dwelling is little more than a hut. The thatch is loose and falling, the walls are wattle and daub. We do not build like him. We build in wood. We build to last.

Tobias and John do the hard work, felling, hauling, and sawing. Joseph, John's oldest son, is thirteen now and works like a man beside his father. Sometimes others come to help them. All must have shelter before the winter. It is important for the settlement. Jonah advises on the building. Our houses differ from the others, on Jonah's instruction. He orders that they be made from solid trunks squared off and fitted together with moss between the layers to fill in the cracks. He has seen this done in Bohemia. It makes the houses snug in winter.

As summer fades to autumn, we look always toward the winter, for the winters here are severe. By then the work must be done or we will freeze to death, our animals with us. John says to build a byre for the animals close to the house, so that they have warmth and shelter. The animals would perish if left outside in field or forest, and they will be easy to get to when the snow is deep, and even to step outside the door will be a test to be endured.

Aside from Martha's chickens, which lay well and prosper, we have a cow now, and swine. Tobias has traded some of his spare tools, and as there is no doctor here, Jonah is an apothecary. People have begun to come to him for treatment, and they pay him in kind.

46.

*Our time has been filled* to brimming with work and still more work, but now the Riverses' house is finished. We all live crammed in there together until the other one can be done.

I have begun to visit the forest to collect moss for the house-building and plants for Jonah. He and Martha are making the Physick Garden. Tobias is fencing it now to keep the hogs out, and they are preparing beds for seeds and planting cuttings brought from home. Sage, thyme, and rosemary are planted in pots so that they can be taken in when the frosts come; feverfew, selfheal, sorrel, tansy, peony, and poppy will be sown in the spring. Jonah's own knowledge is extensive, but he draws on Martha, writing down the things she tells him, things he didn't know.

"What can I tell you, my dear? I'm just a simple countrywoman," Martha says, feigning impatience.

"You know much." Jonah's dark eyes sparkle. "More than many a London doctor of physick."

Martha demurs and blushes, telling him to go his ways, but I can tell she is flattered by his praise. She is keen to help him and has a great store of lore, learned from her mother and her mother before her, but no one has ever written it down till now.

Jonah intends to make a book: *Jonah Morse's Compleat Herbal and Historie of Plants of the Old World and New*. At present this is just a great chaos of papers kept in pasteboard covers. He has been taking plants, drawing and describing them, listing their properties, all his life. He has done this in every country he has visited, and wants to collect here, too.

He wanders the forest, and I go with him. We go by instinct, familiarity, or pick anything curious that might be interesting. Some plants we know already; they only differ slightly from those that grow at home. Others he knows from what the Indians told him on our way here, or are plants that Mr. Tradescant brought back from Virginia. For many we have no guidance, even to the naming of the plants, let alone their properties. These are the ones that interest him. He wants to be the first to record them. He wants his book to be the first to list their virtues and uses.

"That's one of the reasons I came here, Mary. It is my life's work, you see."

## 47

*I do not always go* to the forest with Jonah. Sometimes I go alone. The seasons turn toward full autumn. The days are hot still, but the nights grow colder. Jonah is needed to help with the building, which must be finished before winter comes. The woodland swells with bounty. I go in search of fruits, nuts, mushrooms, anything to add to our stock of food, and I have to confess a terrible thing. I have a very great secret. If anyone discovers it, I will be punished severely.

I have taken to wearing boy's clothing when I venture out alone in the forest.

The paths are close and small. Briar and bramble would snag on my long skirts, snatch off my bonnet, tear my bodice, so I set out to acquire male attire. First I begged a stout leather jerkin from Jonah. He gave it to me freely, saying that he no longer has use for it; it was ever too tight and now is like to split. Next I found a cap belonging to Tobias, which had come from the clothes bundle full of moth holes. He will not need it again as Rebekah is knitting him another. My greatest prize is a pair of Joseph's breeches. He has grown out of them, and Sarah has given them to me to be cut down. But her next son, Joshua, is small of stature and scarce out of petticoats, so I judged that they would not be missed for a good while yet.

I keep all hidden, wrapped in oilskin, in the middle of a hollow tree.

## 48.

*Today was clear and warm*, and I ventured far, farther than I had been before. I wandered until past noon. It was very hot and airless under the trees, and my sack was growing ever heavier. I was thinking of going back, or at least stopping for a time, when I came upon a great pond, so overhung by trees that I almost fell into it.

It looked cool by the water, and I climbed down to where a great smooth rock jutted out like a sunlit platform. I reached down to scoop a drink. The water felt cold, but not chilling, and soft to the touch. I was hot, sweating under my clothes, as I seemed to have been all summer.

The days are warm and we work hard. But there is so little privacy that washing more than hands and face is next to impossible. How many times have I longed for a bath?

I looked around. I had seen no one all morning, and I was miles from the village. I quickly stripped off my clothes and let myself down into the water. It felt smooth, folding round my body like dark green silk. I had no soap but scrubbed myself as best I could, washing my hair and wringing it out. I swam to the middle and let myself float, looking up at the leaves, the sunlight through the trees. When my skin was beginning to pucker with goose flesh, I hauled myself out and lay on the sun-soaked rock.

I must have slept, for when I woke, the sun had changed in the sky. I recollected where I was and grabbed my clothes. As I lifted the bundle, something fell from the top of it. A little bunch of leaves. The leaves had a soapy feel to them, waxy to the touch. I held them tight in my hand. They had not been there before I went into the water. Of that I was sure. I had never seen them before. How did they appear?

I looked around. There was no sign of anyone. Everything was quiet; the lake lay still as a mirror. A sudden cry made me start. It was a jaybird, that was all. The jays here are bright blue, their call softer than ours at home. I looked for the flash of color but saw nothing, just heard the call again. It sounded like laughter as it echoed through the silence of the woods.

I took the little bundle of leaves and stuffed them in my sack.

All the way back I felt as though I was being watched—I felt my skin pricking, and that's a sure sign of it—but I saw nothing. At first I thought that it was someone from the settlement. I hurried to my hollow tree, fearing that I would be discovered, but when men do venture into the forest, to hunt, or cut wood, or fell trees, they make a deal of noise that can be heard for miles. I almost began to believe in spirits.

Jonah was most interested in my new plant. He turned the leaves over in his hands, examining them with his glass, pronouncing it to be some species of soapwort. He thought it could be useful in times when real soap was not available. He asked where I had found it.

"By a lake," I said, the color springing to my face.

"Hmm, hmm. Good, good."

Jonah did not notice my blushes. He spread a sprig carefully and began to copy it into his *Herbal*, making me promise to show him where I found it growing. I nodded in agreement, wondering what I would show him, since I did not find it *growing* at all.

### 49.

The next time that I went to the forest, I felt again the pricking of my skin. I stopped to listen and look around, but I could see no one, hear nothing out of the ordinary. I went on, pretending nonchalance, but with all my senses alert. Still I had no warning.

He appeared so suddenly that I truly thought he *was* a spirit, and I started back, showing fear despite myself.

It was the Indian boy, the one I had seen in Salem, the one who had helped to guide us here. He carried a short bow in one hand and a quiver of arrows slung across his back. He held his other hand out open-palmed toward me, probably thinking that I would bolt from him, crashing away like some startled animal, as Deborah would or Sarah or any of the other girls from the town. But they would never come so far into the forest. They cower on the edge, peering into the trees like frightened children. I am not like them. Once I had gathered my senses, I stood my ground.

"I am not afraid. What do you want?"

He shrugged and looked down. He has lashes long and thick as a girl's; they brush the black lines painted above the markings on his cheeks. Then he looked back up at me, his eyes full of mischief.

"I have seen you many times. I thought you were a boy, at first, but when I left the plant . . ."

If he left the soapwort by the lake, then he must have seen me. . . .

I stared, eyes wide and horrified, far more discomforted by that than by his knife or bow or his fearsome appearance. His laughter rang out, and from somewhere deep in the woods first one jaybird called back, then another. He laughed even more as memory brought the blood thudding to my face. Now I turned to run, but he was too quick for me.

"Stay." He caught my arm. "Our people, the girls and women often go naked—it means nothing."

"It means something to me." I shook him off and ran as fast as I could.

"Wait! Stop!" he called after me. "You and the old man—Jonah—"

I did not hear the rest of his words, I just went on running until I was back at my hollow tree.

## 50.

Jonah has had an accident. He was helping Tobias and John in the saw pit when a log that they were positioning slipped, falling onto his ankle. The foot is at a bad angle, and Martha thinks the bone may be broken, but there is no way of telling as the joint has swollen to prodigious size. She gives him poppy to take the pain away, but she calls for Saint Johnswort, bryony, comfrey, dill, and scabious to make a poultice. None of them grows here. I do not know what to do.

51.

*Martha has done what she can* with her store of medicines, but Jonah's foot blackens and he is feverish. There is no doctor in the settlement. There are only a few of them in the colony, and no one is sure where we would find one willing to come. Not everyone even sees the need for one, despite Jonah's poor condition. Reverend Johnson says the matter is in the hands of God.

Tobias is preparing to ride. We have no horse, but John Rivers has offered his. It is past noon, though, and John thinks that it would be better to start out tomorrow morning. All is undecided, but what we do know is Jonah will lose his foot if he does not get help, and may well die. Martha bites her lip; she thinks we are already too late. I see it in her eyes.

I can stay inside no longer. I will take my sack and head for the forest. Collecting now is not a matter of curiosity merely, of scientific discovery. It is a matter of life or death.

52.

*I took tracks untrodden* and ways unknown. I was not afraid of getting lost. I was brought up in the forest, friend to the woodcutters' sons and the charcoal burners' children; I mark my way.

I did not at first see the Indian boy, but that did not mean he wasn't there. I walked until I felt my skin pricking again. It's a kind of game we've been playing, but now it had to stop.

I called for him to come out.

"What do you want?"

"I need your help." I explained our trouble.

He listened carefully. "My grandfather remembers Jonah. He thinks Jonah's a good man. Not like the others. A healer, like himself. My grandfather is Powwaw." He frowned as he tried to find a way to explain. "More than a healer, spirit leader."

"Like a minister?"

"Not like John Son." He pronounced the parts of the name separately, as if they were two different words. "My grandfather guessed what Jonah did in the forest and sent me to help; I left the soapwort as a gift. Then, when I met you again, you ran away from me."

"Will you help us now?"

"I will ask my grandfather. He will know what is best."

"Take me to him."

"No. That is impossible. I will come to you."

"When?"

"Soon."

He was gone before I could question him more.

## 53

*Jonah is no better.* His fever grows and his foot blackens even more. He has been moved from the Riverses' to the house he is building with Tobias. It is a bare shell, but at least it is quiet and empty of children. Martha tends him, as he tosses and groans. All night the fever grows, and by the morning he is delirious.

I meant to stay awake and help Martha, but I must have dozed off. I awoke to find Tobias pulling on his boots.

Dawn was breaking, the air rang with the sound of birds calling from the forest.

"I wish that bird would stop its chatter." Martha put her fingers to her temples. Through the general chorus came the cry of a jaybird, calling again and again.

I ran to the door, wrenching it open. On one side of the step stood a great basket of herbs. Fleshy stems and thick glossy leaves glistened with dew, so freshly picked that they had not begun to droop. On the other side of the step lay a smaller basket, covered with a cloth. This contained small gourds, little clay pots, and folded packets of bark. I looked up and around. The jaybird call was near, very near. I followed into the forest.

He was waiting for me under the trees. There he gave me his grandfather's instructions. The leaves in the basket must be boiled and the cooling mass bound around the foot. The powders in the birch bark folds must be mixed in water and drunk to control the fever. The liquid in the clay pots is to clear the blood of poisons. Lastly the contents of the little gourds should be rubbed onto the skin to help heal the break once the bone is set and the swelling gone down.

I don't know how to thank him.

"He is not cured yet. I will be here tomorrow to see how he does. Listen for me."

"Wait! What is your name?"

"Jaybird—can't you guess?"

His laugh rang out and birds replied from all around the forest.

When I went back to the cabin, Martha had taken the baskets inside. She had guessed the purpose of the bunches of leaves and was boiling them in a kettle. The smell they gave was clean and fresh, conquering the odors of sickness, filling the room with healing.

I told her how I had come by these things, and explained the treatment carefully. Martha is not happy about the extent of my woodland wandering, less so about trafficking with the natives and using their heathen remedies. The proof of the pudding will be in the eating. She knows we have no choice.

Tobias does not need to go for the doctor. The poultice has eased the swelling, and the powders have brought the fever down. The color of the skin is improving. Jonah's foot is no longer black.

"'Tis a miracle," Martha said as she unwrapped the dressing. "That's what it is. We are all God's children. They are better Christians than some I could name, despite their heathen ways." She turns to me. "'Tis not to say I'm pleased with how you came by this. Such wandering could draw attention. If you were seen . . . and with *him* . . ."

"But I have been most careful not to be."

"But if you *were* . . ."

She looks at me, her honest face troubled, but she leaves off scolding to tend to Jonah. His pain is not over. Martha and I prepare to set the bones. We will need Tobias to hold him down.

### 54.

*I have to heed Martha's grumbling.* I have limited my visits to the forest, but still I go. Our only neighbors are the Riverses, not counting old Tom Carter— and he's either drunk or in a stupor. I never see anyone else, so what do they know?

Anyway, Jonah thinks Martha's fears are silly. He encourages me to find out more. Sumac, sassafras, snakeweed, joe-pye weed, pipsissewa, snakeroot, skullcap. The list grows. Jaybird shows me where to find the healing plants and herbs, giving some their native names, others the names that the settlers give to them. He explains the properties of the plants, pointing out which parts are poisonous, which are wholesome, what can be used to treat which ailments. I listen carefully so that I can tell Jonah.

"How does he do?"

"Much better. Soon he will be able to walk with a stick. Meanwhile he sits with his leg propped up and works on his *Herbal*."

"I told my grandfather about that. He finds what you do interesting. He wants to meet you."

"You mean Jonah. But he can't walk, I told you."

"Not him. You."

"Why me?"

"That's for him to tell you."

"When?"

"Not today. It grows late. You will know when. I will find you."

With that he left, melting into the forest. I know I cannot follow. I cannot even tell which direction he takes. His feet make no sound, no scuffing of leaves or cracking of twigs, and I catch no sight of him in the dappled shadows.

## 55.

*I never know* if Jaybird will be there. He just appears. I never see him. He could be an arm's length away and I would not guess it. He is teaching me how to be quiet in the woods. Quiet enough for the animals to come out and show no fear. And he teaches me bird-calls. I can do the jaybird almost as well as he does. That's how I know he's there. I call, and he calls back.

Sometimes he leaves gifts by our door. Little woven baskets of rush or willow, containing nuts and fruit, plums and blueberries. He knows that blueberries are Martha's favorite; they are like bilberries but sweeter and bigger. Martha exclaims, and worries that he might be seen, but I can tell by her face that she is pleased.

He never comes to the town. Neither do any other native people. He is the only one I have seen since we came here.

## 56. October 1659

"*You want to know why* the woods are empty of my people?"

We are eating strawberries in the forest. Jaybird knows a place where the fruits grow until the first

160

snow, which will not be long now. We sit opposite each other. Dressing like a boy makes me easier with him. He treats me like a brother.

"I will tell you. When the first settlers came, my people welcomed them, and without us they would have perished. We taught them how to live, what to grow, when to sow, when to harvest. We thought the land was big enough for all to live together. But that was not to be. More came, and more came, wanting more land and more land. They took the land, land that we had cleared, for it was easier for them to settle there. But that was not what killed the people."

"You were attacked? Wiped out?"

He shook his head. "Not in the way you mean, with guns and weapons. The white man brought sickness, disease. This began many years ago, before even the first pilgrims came to Plymouth. Fishermen began to come from Europe, to fish the seas in the north. Every winter they went back, but they did not have to stay to leave their fevers behind. Then traders came, wanting fur, and they too brought illness. When the English came they brought the spotted sickness. Our medicine men were powerless against these sicknesses they had never seen, that came from across the sea.

"Many, many of our people died. Those that were left were too weak to hunt, to fish, to plant crops or bring in the harvest. We belonged to the Pentucket tribe of the Pennacook nation. Our main village was to the north, on the Merrimack River. So few were left there that their land was sold to the English. My father was a sachem, leader of a small band remote from the main center, on a tributary river. He hoped that his band could escape the sickness, which raged along the Merrimack, but that was not to be. People came to us for help and brought the sickness with them. He died, and my mother, and my sister and brothers, and many, many others. A white man, a good man, took pity on our plight. He did what he could for the sick, which was little, and he took me and some others. Cared for us, schooled us, treated us as his own."

"But you left him?"

"The choice was not a hard one to make. I grew old enough to know that there is more to being a white man than learning his language and wearing his clothes. I wanted to go home to my people." His fingers went up and touched the black tortoise-shaped tattoo marked out on his cheek. "Except I found that I had no home, I had no people. My village was a white man's town. Beulah."

"What had happened? Where had they gone?"

"We do not live just in one place as the white man does. The place you call Beulah was our place in summer. In winter we go deeper into the forest to hunt and take shelter from the worst of the weather, and we come back in the spring to plant and fish. It has always been that way. One spring the people—those who were left—returned, to find the village had been taken. Their holy places overturned. The graves of their ancestors desecrated and built upon. Their food stores had been broken open, the contents stolen. They had no choice but to move on."

"So there was no one?"

"Just my grandfather. He stayed. He watches the holy places. The stones are still there . . ."

"What stones?"

"Great stones stood on the top of the hill. They had been there since time began, marking the place as sacred to our people, and now . . ."

"They lie under our Meeting House."

I remember remarking how oddly shaped they were, not fresh-cut and squared, but ancient, weathered by time, worn by wind and rain.

"We have stones like that at home." I told him of the ones my grandmother visited, and the great ones I had seen on Salisbury Plain.

"Then your people should respect them."

It was my turn to shake my head. "They would think them heathen."

"Even their own?"

"Even their own. You have been in the town?"

"Enough times."

He did not explain, but I could tell from the way he said it that he would not go again.

## 57.

"There's been talk. I told you there would be." Martha fixed her eye upon me.

Our house is finished. After we have eaten we settle round the fire as darkness descends outside. Martha had a visit this day from her sister, which always unsettles her.

"Talk?" I looked up from my stitching. "Of what?"

"Of you. Wandering in the forest. And more besides."

"What talk is this, Martha?" Jonah asked, alerted by the worry in Martha's voice.

"Jethro Vane complains his hogs sicken. He says that someone has given them the Evil Eye. Mary was seen to come and go from the place where they roam. And she was seen staring at them and shouting, like to cursing . . ."

"I was not cursing! You told me to drive them off if they came in our garden! I was shouting because they are bold creatures, half wild from living in the woods. They take some shifting."

"Who told you this?" Jonah interrupted.

"My sister, Anne Francis. She wanted to warn me, what folks were saying . . ."

"Worry you more like." Jonah's face darkened. "She strikes me as a meddler and a keen bearer of ill tidings. Take no notice."

"Not much gets past our Annie. She has an ear for gossip, that I'll give you, and a finger into every pie." Martha shook her head. "But that only serves to strengthen her warning. You do not know these people as I do."

"That's as may be, but there's always some proper explanation." He sighed. " 'Evil Eye'? What stuff!" Jonah is a man of science and has little truck with superstition. "Like as not Jethro Vane's swine caught the sickness from the ones his brother brought here." He went back to his book. "They looked to me like a sickly lot."

"Like as not they caught it from Jeremiah himself," I said.

Tobias laughed. Jeremiah Vane shares his daughter Deborah's coloring. He is russet-bearded, small-eyed, narrow-jawed, and long-snouted, and thus much resembles a Tamworth hog.

"This is no matter for laughing!" Martha's eyes flared green in warning. "Such talk is dangerous. We all know where such whispers lead. We don't want folk turning against us." She turned to Tobias. "You, sir,

165

can mend the fencing. I do not want his hogs anywhere near our property. And you"—it was my turn
now—"you can mend your ways! No more going into
the forest. No more wandering lest tongues wag even
more."


58.

"*They live in the forest* in nakedness, in sin and
degradation. They make nothing of the land. They
live worse than beggars."

Goodwife Anne is paying another visit, this time
in the evening, so she can speak to all of us. She is giving us newcomers the benefit of her wisdom and supe-
rior experience. Her subject is the native people.

Martha sits, face closed. If it was not for the native
people her sister so despises, Jonah would be in his
grave by now. Her eyes flick up, warning us to say
nothing. Jonah draws the sprig on the table in front of
him. Tobias sits in the corner, whittling a doll for
Rebekah's sister. I want to shout, cry out about how
little she understands. The Indians go lightly in the
world, that is all. They make their homes from living
trees, only taking what they need before moving on to
let the land replenish itself. But I hold my tongue.
Goody Francis is a stupid, narrow-minded, ignorant,

166

busybody of a woman, poking her long nose into everything, puffing out her saggy cheeks to make judgments, then pulling her mouth in like a tightly drawn purse string.

"What is it that you write, child? May I see?"

My fingers jerked, splaying the nib cut into the quill, turning the *g* I was forming into a crooked blot.

"Mary helps me." Jonah handed me a knife to cut a new nib, which I did though my hand was trembling. "With my *Herbal.*"

"May I see?"

Goody Francis stretched out her hand.

Jonah made a show of sorting through the papers in front of him, spreading them out to cover my writing. She clearly meant for me to give her what I was writing, but Jonah gave her his book instead. She took it from him. She opened the pasteboard covers. The pages crackled and buckled as she turned them. She studied what she found there carefully, brows knit, as if she understood what she looked at, but her mouth worked to form the words, and her finger ran under the writing, marking her as almost unlettered.

"What is this?"

She had stopped at *mandrake, mandragora.* The drawing of the root looks like a small man, a homunculus. At the base of the trunk, the root forked, split into three parts. She fairly shrieked at it, shrilling her disgust.

"It looks like a poppet, a waxen image." She shuddered. "Unclean!"

Jonah's eyes twinkled. "No more so than a carrot or parsnip."

Her thin lips pursed and puffed, slowly spelling over the letters describing the plant's purpose, and her putty face paled even more.

"I have heard stories about this root. It grows only under the gallows tree and screams like a human thing when pulled from the ground."

"All false and untrue. Old wives' tales. Doltish dreams put about by runagate surgeons and physick mongers. The root has many virtues. It provokes sleep, eases pain. Have a care what you believe, Mistress."

"Have a care what you write in your book." She snapped the covers shut. "Such are kept by magicians and folk of that sort, up to the Devil's work."

"I am an apothecary." He took the book back from her. "It is necessary for me to keep a record of the virtues of plants and different simples and cures."

Goody Francis folded her arms across her black bodice and set her mouth in a stubborn line.

"Such stuff smacks of magic."

Jonah sighed. "Not so, Goody Francis, not so. You did not complain when I dressed your husband's leg when he cut it on the scythe. This is where I found the herbs to heal the wound and ease the pain. I am the closest thing to a doctor here. I have kept this book all my life. I need it for my practice and will not stop now."

Goody Francis did not looked convinced, but she would not better Jonah. She turned on me instead.

"You may say what you please, Master Morse, but inky fingers on a girl are very far from natural. You've been making far too free." She looked from me over to where her sister sat sewing. "You would be better set staying close and helping Martha. Take it from me."

She paused and sat up straighter, sucking in her breath and then puffing out her cheeks and chest, so obviously readying herself for some pronouncement that even Tobias looked up.

"I have to tell you, sister"—she turned to address Martha—"that this, this arrangement"—she waved one hand around to indicate the room, our home—"this arrangement has been called into question."

"'Called into question'?" Jonah looked up. "How so?"

"Some think that it is not fitting that a young girl should share a house with men who are not related to her."

She glanced at Jonah, at the pages in front of him. If he had been suspect before, this made him more so.

"Who says this?" Martha's voice trembled. "We live as a family here."

"Just so." Goody Francis gave her little pursed smile. "And you live in error. It would be much more suitable if this girl"—she waved her hand toward me—"lived with the Riverses. They are a proper family. It has been brought to the attention of the Reverend Johnson."

"By whom, may I ask?" Martha's hands were trembling as she put aside her sewing. I could see her temper rising.

"The Reverend will talk with the selectmen. You will be told what they decide."

At that she rose to go.

"Wait, mistress." Jonah's face was creased with concern. "Do we not have a say in this?"

"Newcomers have no say as yet."

"What about the Riverses; do *they* have no say? It's their household she'd be joining."

"They will abide by the decision. John Rivers is a God-fearing man. How can it be otherwise?" She spoke with drawn-out patience, as if addressing a pack of ignorant children. "With the Reverend Johnson's strength and under his guidance, the meeting always comes to the right decision. God speaks through them; how else could we know of His intention? The will of the meeting is the will of all."

## 59

*As soon as her sister had left*, Martha fell to scolding me and Jonah about what we put in our books. Goody Francis could not read better than an infant, I said, so I hardly saw that it mattered, but Martha shook her head and pointed out that this place doesn't lack scholars and they could soon be sending those who can.

Ever the gleeful bearer of bad tidings, Goody Francis returned to tell us that I am, indeed, to pack my box and move next door. It took no more than a couple days for this to be brought about, and Goody Francis is exceedingly pleased about it. Martha is more than a little unhappy, but she thinks that it may be for the best. She does not want more suspicion to fall on me, and thinks I will be safer with Rebekah and her family. For me it is no hardship. Rebekah is as a sister, and if I look on Martha as a mother, then Sarah Rivers is a favorite aunt. John Rivers is a good man, wise and fair-minded. It is no imposition to live with them, but I do not like being shifted like a piece on a chessboard.

## 60.  Late October 1659

*Although it is late autumn,* the days stay clear, blue, and brilliant. The woods are full of color. At home the leaves change; here they flame. I long to escape, but there is much to do and I have promised Martha not to go beyond the settlement boundaries.

The houses are finished, but there is still work to be done to make them comfortable. They are small, two rooms below and one long one above, but more rooms can be added if need be. The Riverses' house is slightly larger, which is a good thing as they must find room for me as well now.

When we are not working in the house, we help our neighbors with their harvest, and there is wood to be cut for the winter to come.

## 61.

*The days grow ever shorter.* The birds fly south. Great skeins of duck and geese sketch jagged lines in the sky, morning and night, their high drawn-out calls like the cries of lost souls.

I listen to them and wonder. I have seen nothing of Jaybird for weeks. Perhaps he and his grandfather have left already. Perhaps they too journey south.

## 62. November 1659

*The mornings still dawn blue* and brilliant, but ice glazes the water barrel, and the ground is dusted with rime. Winter comes on and we are ready. The crops are harvested, the houses finished. Wood stands up to the eaves on either side of the doorway.

The late autumn weather is fickle. It could snow any day, or so John Rivers has been told. After breakfast I took my sack and set out for the forest. It might be my last chance before the snow comes. I know what I promised Martha, but since I no longer live with her, I convince myself that her prohibition no longer holds.

Mist crept up from the hollows, and my legs disappeared up to my knees. It was like wading through freshly carded wool. The sun was low, scarce above the horizon. It cast a strange light, catching on scarlet leaves hanging from twigs and branches. It looked as though the trees dripped blood.

I marked my path in the way I learned from the woodcutters and charcoal men, with cuts and notches and bending branches. The woods were very quiet this morning. Unnaturally so. I felt my skin pricking again. I stood quite still for a long time, studying each area, committing it to memory, looking for the slightest change, in the way Jaybird has taught me, but when the raucous call erupted from a bush almost in front of me, it still made me jump.

He came out laughing and the birds cackled back.

"You must look near as well as far. My grandfather wants to see you. Come."

We journeyed a long way, and not to any encampment. At noon we stopped and shared the food we had brought with us. I had bread and cheese; he had nuts and strips of dried deer meat.

We went on up a long narrow valley with steep walls on either side, strewn with fallen trees. A stream rushed at our feet, the water white with tumbling over the rocks. We climbed toward a notch in the hills. Here the stream turned to a waterfall, cascading over ledges of rock as smooth and regular as descending pavement. I looked to Jaybird, wondering what we were to do here. He smiled and pointed up. I was by no means sure that this feat could be accomplished; from the bottom such an ascent seemed sheer. But it was not as difficult as I thought, although I was glad to be wearing breeches—in a skirt such a climb would have been impossible. The ledges afforded a kind of narrow and slippery staircase. Jaybird helped me over the most difficult parts of it, counselling me to take it easy, one bit at a time, and not to look down until we had reached the top. Only once did I glance past my feet to see boulders rendered to pebbles, the stream like a thread of twine.

I was more worried about what was above.

Over our heads the ledges of rock jutted out, one above another, like books stacked in a pile about to topple. The ones at the bottom sloped inward, but then the angle was reversed. At the top, water fell over a wide overhang. I could not see how we could possibly climb that.

Jaybird stepped sideways, indicating for me to follow him onto a shelf of rock. The water fell in a crystal curtain. We were behind the waterfall now. The air was dank, the rock wet and slippery but wide enough to walk along easily. The wall was covered in mosses and ferns. We edged along it until we came to a deep recess. Jaybird stepped into the darkness. We had come to a cave.

The inside was dimly lit. Light filtered through the screening water, playing on the walls, creating shimmering shadows. It was like being in a cavern under the sea. Jaybird went to a niche and brought out a torch, a pine branch topped with a ball of resin. He struck a flint and the torch burned to show the recesses of the cave. The chamber narrowed, branching into several tunnels. Jaybird led me into one on the right. I followed the smoky light, gripping on tightly to his hand. The tunnels twisted and turned like a maze. I knew that I could never find my way out on my own.

We walked for a long time, until the torch was burned down and sputtering, then gradually the darkness in front began to lighten and there seemed to be more space around us. The cave was opening out into a lofty chamber, and from the center came the flicker of firelight.

We had walked right through the mountain. It had been so dark in the tunnels that I had almost persuaded myself it was night. Now I emerged into afternoon sun striking golden over a broad country, clothed in trees like tapestry. We were very high up. Below me the mountain fell away in a headlong precipice, and the land spread out in front of me. Here and there, hills and crags showed, but the blanketing trees seemed to stretch forever, as far as the eye could see, merging into the violet mist smudging the curving horizon.

"This place is special for my people."

Indeed, the cave was like a cathedral. The pale gray walls soared in ribbed curtains and delicate vaulted columns that owed nothing to man's artistry.

"It stays the same here, winter and summer." He stirred the fire. "We are sheltered from the wind and snow. The cave faces south, so it gets what sun there is, and it is so high up that a fire cannot be seen from below. The smoke rises, escaping up into the chambers where no man can see it. Sometimes a bear blunders in, but once he sees the place is taken, he goes. We have what we need to stay all winter long."

I looked around. There were beds made from springy firs and soft mosses overlaid with thick furs. Baskets and clay pots lined the walls. But there seemed to be no one else there. No sign of his grandfather.

As if my thoughts had called him, the old man stepped out of the shadows.

He spoke in his own language. And the boy replied, "I have brought her."

The old man said something. It sounded like a name, but not one I can render on paper.

"What did he say?"

"It is his name for you: *mahigan shkiizhig*. It is what he calls you: Eyes of a Wolf."

"Why does he call me that?"

"Why? It is just as my laugh is like the jaybird call, and I love to wear bright things. My grandfather is White Eagle, because of his hair and the feather he wears. So you have the eyes of a wolf."

I frowned, trying to understand his meaning. The only wolves that I had ever seen were heads hammered to the Meeting House, and those eyes were glazed with death or eaten out by maggots.

"You have no wolves in your country?"

"Perhaps in the north, in Scotland, but not in England—they have all been killed."

Jaybird told his grandfather, who shook his head. Jaybird turned back to me.

"He says that is bad."

"Why?" I asked. "They kill the sheep and lambs, children sometimes, and they can attack a man."

The old man shrugged and spoke.

Jaybird nodded. "He says everything has its own place in the world, wolves and men."

The old man spoke again.

"You remind him of a young she-wolf he knew once. She was fierce, proud, and brave but not fully grown into her strength. She lived on the edge of the pack, rejected by them but forced to go back because she was not old enough to survive without them. He feels the same fierce pride in you. You want to bow to no one, but you are young, and life on the edge is uncomfortable."

"What happened to her, the young she-wolf?"

The old man replied, but the boy seemed reluctant to translate his grandfather's words.

"What did he say?"

"He wants to know about the hare."

"Hare? What hare?"

What was he talking about? Some of the settlers think the Indians mad as moonstruck calves. Perhaps they are right.

"He has seen a hare in the forest and on the land around your village. It was not there before. It appeared suddenly when you and your people came."

"Do you not have hares in this country?" I asked, rather as he had asked me about the wolves.

"Of course we do. And the Great Hare is very important in the stories of our people; that is why my grandfather noticed. He thought it a sign from the Great Hare to him."

The old man nodded. He had been following the conversation. He understood English even if he did not speak it.

"This hare," the boy went on, "is different from the hares who live here. It is smaller and a different color."

Across the fire, the old man's eyes caught mine. Twin points of flame flickered red in their depths. Suddenly my grandmother came sitting into my mind. She was there completely, as if stories about in the cave next to me. I remember ge herself into a her, how they said that she cou ever said whether it hare. She had never spoken uch that she had never was true or not. There been waiting until I was told me; perhaps ever came. I remembered her in older, but that eyes shut but not sleeping, lying as the bed next How did I know where she went? still as if

A then there was the story Jack had told me, ab the rabbit on the ship. Hare or rabbit. I had aughed, but the sailors feared it. . . .

The old man said something to the boy.

"He says you know."

"But what is my grandmother doing here? Why does she choose a hare?"

"Your grandmother's spirit takes the form of a hare because it is her animal—just as yours is the wolf, his is the eagle, and mine is the blue jay."

"Is such a thing possible?"

The old man looked at me as if I doubted the existence of moonlight or the sunrise. He waved his hands, weaving them above his head. Flames leapt upward and I saw that the walls of the cave were covered with pictures of animals: some were little more than squares and ...les, others were recognizable as deer with great hu... antlers, bear, wolf, lion, and horned and them w... creatures that I could not name. With naked, some ...—hunting, stalking, dancing—some drawn in charcoa... in skins. Some of the images were cut into the rock. T...rs painted in vivid colors, others man's arms seemed to br...ate movements of the old men danced to the flutter of ...m to life. Animals and flicker. They moved across the w...ds in the firelight's mals, sometimes men, sometimes both...sometimes animals, ... same time.

"This is the place of our ancestors," ... the boy explained. "Here we are surrounded by their pre...ce."

Again I had the feeling of being in a great chur..., a place filled with spirit, like the Temple of the Winds on Salisbury Plain, heavy with the presence of those who had gone before.

I told them about my grandmother and what had happened to her.

The old man spoke again.

"What does he say?"

"Her spirit is restless because of the great wrong done to her. It has followed you across the ocean."

"Why? For what purpose?"

The old man stared into the fire. It was some time before he spoke to the boy, but when he did speak, it was at some length. The boy listened carefully, nodding to show that he remembered and would render the old man's words exactly.

"To warn, to watch over, to ask for vengeance. He is not sure. Just as the physical form is different from the creatures native here, so the spirit is foreign to him; so he cannot be certain. He says that to take such a journey shows great love or great fear or both. He thinks she is here because she fears for you. That which was done to her could be done to you."

That was the end of the audience. The old man rose in one fluid movement. He lit a taper from the fire and went to the far wall. Here he drew back a blanket, finely woven in stripes and lines and intricate designs, and went into a room carved into the rock.

Jaybird led me back through the caves, this time a different way.

"What did he say about the young she-wolf? Did he say what happened to her?" I asked when we finally emerged into the fading afternoon.

"He did not know. One day she was not there anymore. Maybe the pack drove her out, or . . ."

"Or what?"

"Or maybe they turned on her and tore her to pieces."

A far from auspicious story. No wonder he did not want to tell me. Perhaps the old man was mistaken. Perhaps it is all in his imagination, a figment of native superstition.

We were quite a distance from the settlement, but I could hear the baying of dogs, and men crashing through the woods.

"Hunters from Beulah," Jaybird said.

"How do you know?"

"They are the only white men for miles around. My people make no sound. I will have to leave you. Make sure they don't see you. Your clothes."

I had forgotten that I was dressed like a boy.

"When will I see you again?"

"Spring, perhaps. Or summer."

"So long?"

"Soon we will be in the grip of winter. And Mohawks raid to the west and north. There is war, and rumor of war. The people are scattered. My grandfather travels to meet his brothers, to find out what is happening to them."

"War? It has not been mentioned in the settlement."

"Why would it be? It is Indian killing Indian. White men take no interest in that."

### 63.  Late November 1659

*Tobias goes out to hunt* in the woods. He goes with two young men about his own age: Josiah Crompton, the son of one of the old settlers, and Ned Cardwell, Jethro Vane's hired man. Perhaps they were the huntsmen Jaybird and I had heard, although they made so much noise it would be a wonder if they caught anything, and Tobias and his friends seem very successful.

Today I met them as they came out of the woods, carrying turkeys and geese slung over their shoulders. Their dogs panted along by their sides, two rough-coated spaniels and a brindled hound. The dogs were filthy, mud caking their flanks, leaving only a narrow clean stripe down their backs. Tobias does not have a dog of his own. Dogs are not as common here as they are at home.

"You did well."

I joined them as they walked back, our steps quickening toward the low squat houses of the town. Although the hour was not late, night drew on apace. Smoke curled from the chimneys, spreading up into a sky heavy and gray, tinged yellowish at the edges with the closing day. The curfew bell sounds at dusk. All must be in by then; to be abroad is to be a nightwalker, and that is a crime. Another of the regulations that rule the town.

"Aye." Tobias held up his trophies. "A turkey for Martha and a goose for Sarah."

"Give her a goose and you'll be invited for supper." One of the young men winked at him.

Tobias smiled back. The understanding between him and Rebekah is well-known.

"We could have done better yet. Coursed a hare down in the south meadow. Haven't seen one hereabouts before. Old 'un, I reckon. Held itself odd, head awry, but it moved sprightly enough."

"You did not catch it?"

"No." Josiah Crompton shook his head. "Outran old Tom, here." He pointed to the hound walking at our side. "Got away into the woods."

I leaned down, intending to scratch the patch of fur that was free of mud on the top of his long bony head.

"Careful, missy. He don' take to strangers," his owner warned, but what happened then surprised even me.

As soon as the dog's amber eyes met mine, its forehead began wrinkling and it set to whining. It sat down, head on paws, ears back, rump wiggling, tail wagging, then it rolled over to show its mud-caked underbelly.

"Well, well, I'll be damned!" Josiah Crompton tipped back his hat to scratch his head. "Never done that afore. In general, he's a fierce old boy."

"Got an eye for a pretty girl; that's the way of it!" Ned Cardwell leered at me.

"No call for that." Tobias put a brotherly arm round me, shepherding me away from them. "Come, Mary. Martha will be fretting and Sarah will be wondering where you have got to."

## 64.

*The wolves are back.* Last night I heard them, and the night before.

The wind blows from the north.

"There's snow at the back of it." That's what Jonah says.

It is time for the beasts to come in from the fields. Jonah and Tobias have gone with John Rivers to herd them. I am in Martha's house. Next door children tumble everywhere, and I need peace to write my Journal. I write by firelight as she bakes. It is hard to know

185

what time it is. The light is dim in here; the windows are covered in greased paper. We couldn't afford glass, even if there were any to be had.

It seems darker than it should be. It cannot be much past noon. I open the door and see flakes falling, as large and delicate as downy breast feathers. They begin in ones and twos, slow and graceful. I call Martha to come and see. She bustles over, wiping her hand on her apron, curious to know what I am fussing about.

We look up at the sky, at the flakes whirling toward us, faster and faster.

"The old lady is plucking her geese again," she said, and then glanced over her shoulder, a look both quick and furtive. Such superstitions are frowned upon here, and Martha is fearful, even if there is no one to overhear her.

By late afternoon the snow has thickened to a whirling, turbulent mass of white on gray, making it hard to see beyond a few feet. It covers quickly, and as yet, there is no sign of John, or Jonah and Tobias. Rebekah just came to ask if we have seen them. Flakes billow in as Martha trips back and fore to the door like a worried old hen. She looks out anxiously, fretting in case they have lost their way or fallen into a drift or some such. I point out that it has not been snowing long enough for that, but she will not rest until she sees her menfolk back safe at home.

Now Tobias and Jonah struggle up the path, one side white, holding their hats on, squinting from under the brims as the snow drives into their faces. The beasts are similarly covered, snow lying thick upon them like a second pelt. Rebekah asks where her father is. They tell us he is still out looking for sheep. He must find them and pen them. They will be lost in drifts if left to wander, for the snow here can lie very deep.

They leave us to settle the animals in the byre. They have to go back out to help him.

### 65.

*Sheep are stupid creatures.* Without dogs to herd them, they scatter; gathering them up is a difficult business. Most were got back safe, but two were found the next morning, half devoured, their blood staining the fresh snow.

### 66.

*There is no heat* in the Meeting House. Breath steams and streams from our nostrils, glazing the walls and fogging the frosty air.

The Reverend Johnson took the sheep for the theme of his sermonizing, as limbs lost all feeling, noses and cheeks grew numb.

"'All we like sheep have gone astray . . .'"

I dislike being compared to a sheep the most, of all God's creatures.

"'Like sheep they are laid in the grave; death shall feed upon them...'

"The Elders which are among you I exhort . . ."

He looked to the front rank where the Elders sat before him, black clad, still and unmoving, as if carved from coal.

"'Feed the flock of God . . . And when the chief shepherd shall appear, ye shall receive a crown of glory . . .

"'Likewise, ye younger, submit yourself unto the elder . . .'"

His gaze shifted to the rows behind and to the side, where children sat, boys with their fathers, girls with their mothers. They will find no difficulty in obeying this instruction. Stubborn or rebellious behavior toward a parent is a hanging offense.

"'Yea, all of you be subject one to another, and be clothed with humility: for God resisteth the proud and giveth grace to the humble.'"

His gaze took in all of us, his eyes hooded and unblinking.

"'Be sober, be vigilant; because your adversary the Devil, as a roaring lion, walketh about, seeking whom he may devour.'"

The eye ranging over us is as fierce as the one painted on the pulpit.


## 67. December 1659

*Winter sets in like a siege.* The snow lies piled to the eaves, and each day is more bitter than the last. The world outside is reduced to gray, black, and white. We are confined inside for much of the time, never moving far, only crossing the few yards between Martha's house and ours.

The days shorten toward Christmas, except there is no Christmas here. It will be another working day, no different in any way, except, of course, if it falls on the Sabbath.

Rebekah and I cross the space often. I go to see Martha, but Rebekah goes to be with Tobias. They sit off in a corner, murmuring to each other. Away from the circle of the fire, the room is perishing, but they would rather freeze and keep the privacy the darkness affords them. Martha is supposed to act as chaperone, but she is tolerant of lovers who want to be alone. Rebekah often accompanies Tobias when he goes to see to the animals in their byre next to the house.

Martha and I are making a quilt for their marriage bed. We match pieces of cloth from Martha's stock. Tobias has made a frame for her, and Martha has begged wool from those who keep sheep, adding to what she has gathered from hedge and thicket. I have helped her wash and card it to make the padding. What we lack will be made up by old blankets, rags, shirts, and stockings holey and worn beyond repair.

The backing cloth is pegged to the frame, the packing laid, the top put on the other two layers. Martha has marked the top out for stitching. She chose the patterns, sketching them on with a bit of chalk: roses such as grew in her garden, the acorns and oak leaves of the woods round her village, kisses for true love, hearts for the marriage, snails and spirals circling round and round in never closing eternity. We work from the center out, finishing with an unending vine that will twist round the border and must not be broken for it denotes long life.

Rebekah is not allowed to help. Rebekah laughs and says that she will do the same for me when she is an old married lady. She teases me. She has changed lately, no longer shy and reserved but smiling and laughing, her cheeks flushed and eyes sparkling. She is like another girl.

## 68. January 1660

*It is January* and the cold grows worse, bringing with it cruel afflictions. Kibes and chilblains we had at home, but here feet and fingers can become so gnawed by frost that the flesh rots. Besides ordinary coughs and rheum, there is a lung sickness that has some spitting blood. Jonah has been so busy visiting the sick and dispensing remedies that he has fallen ill himself.

Sickness has taken a toll on the Sabbath congregation, and this Sunday there are even more empty spaces. Elias Cornwell is not there, and Reverend Johnson must preach alone. His wife, Goody Johnson, is missing, along with half a row of her little ones.

After the service Martha was summoned to Reverend Johnson.

"You are to attend my wife."

"She is sick?" Martha looked alarmed. Goody Johnson is big with child.

"Not her. Some of the children are unwell."

"What ails them?"

Reverend Johnson looked at a loss, as if he did not concern himself with the ailments of children.

"That is for you to discover."

"I mean how do they suffer? Do they have fever? Do they cough?"

"Cough. Yes. They cough so we get no sleep. I can hardly think. I want you to put a stop to it."

"I'll do what I can. Mary—" Martha turned, about to tell me to go and get her basket.

"You are Mary?" The Reverend Johnson's gun-barrel eyes were trained on me.

"Yes, sir."

"Mary? The orphan girl who lives with John and Sarah Rivers?"

I nodded.

"I have heard about you."

"Heard what, sir? Good report, I hope."

"Not entirely." He stroked his beard. "I have heard that you wander the woods."

"Only to gather herbs and plants for Jonah and Martha."

"I have also heard that you have much to say for yourself. Tell me, Mary. Do you shun the Devil and all his works?"

"I do, sir."

"Do you believe in God? Do you live by His Word?"

"Yes. Yes, of course." I nodded vigorously. What is this catechism?

"Let us hope that you do. For I am His representative here in this community. Do not forget that. There is nothing, nothing that I do not know about." He thought for a moment. "Are you obedient?"

"Yes, sir." I kept my eyes down, trying to look suitably submissive.

"Make sure that you are. Remember: 'Rebellion is as the sin of witchcraft,' so it is written in the Book of Samuel. See to the children, Martha. I do not want to hear them tonight."

He left us without another glance.

69.

*The Reverend Johnson's house* is the largest in the settlement. It is as big as some I saw in Salem, standing two stories high, built out at the sides and roofed with gables. Goody Johnson has asked us to come every day until the children are better.

Martha treats the Reverend Johnson's children with a linctus of coltsfoot and licorice boiled in honey with a touch of vinegar. She rubs their chests with goose grease, binds them with flannel, and makes them breathe steam from a kettle in which she infuses leaves from the forest: pipsissewa, bergamot, native mints.

The children are recovering. The congestion is easing. They will soon be better. It is Goody Johnson herself who worries Martha. Apart from where the great bulge of the baby shows, she is very thin. Martha is concerned that carrying a child may be sapping her beyond her endurance.

## 70

*Winter bites hard* into the lives of all of us. The cold is unrelenting. It is colder if anything, and food is getting scarcer, fresh food scarcest of all. The forest bounty is frozen and buried under snow. Jonah fears scurvy may break out as it did on the ship. His stock of lemon juice is all but exhausted.

The men go out to hunt when they can, but the game has fled the woods hereabouts, and what they do manage to catch is hide and bone.

What we can spare, we share. I have been summoned by Goody Johnson. Martha offers to go herself, but Goody Johnson says that I must go, that Martha will not do. She has a favor to ask of me.

## 71

*Goody Johnson welcomes me in.* Her eyes are huge in her head, and as she smiles, her skin stretches back to show the skull beneath her skin. I have brought tonic for her, from Martha, but fear it will do little good. It is as though the child inside is feeding off her, consuming her to the very bones.

She is a good woman and knows our stores are low. The children have recovered well, and she wants to show her gratitude. She loads me down with gifts of food, which we share among all of us. Corn, peas, beans, oatmeal, loaves she has baked, and even a few precious apples, their skins wizened, but their flavor the sweeter for it.

"Now, the favor." She takes my hand; hers are cold and so thin, the skin stretched to transparency. "The Reverend Johnson's nephew Elias is busy compiling his *Book of Wonders*, but the cold causes painful swelling of the joints in his hands, making it difficult for him to write. I have been scribing for him, but my strength often fails me. He tells me that you can read and write and have a fair hand, and will make a tolerable substitute. Are you willing? If you come, of course, you can eat here, and I'll make sure you have something to take home with you."

How could I refuse? She has given me enough to feed us for a week.


### 72.

*I do not see* the Reverend Johnson often when I visit, and I am glad of it. I did not like the way he questioned me. His strange catechism made me nervous. He never eats with his family and keeps to a separate part of the house, as far from the noise of the children as possible. When I do see him, he ignores me, as if I am beneath his notice.

Elias Cornwell has his own study, a little room tucked at the top of a set of winding stairs. It is small and dark with wood paneling. A fire glows in the grate, and good candles stand on a table strewn with papers. It is here that he works on his pamphlet. It began as the journal he kept aboard ship but is now to be called: *A Book of Miracles, Providential Wonders, and Many Remarkable Things (which may probably come to pass)*, by Elias Cornwell.

I think the title too long, but do not see it as my place to remark upon it.

He hopes to travel to Boston in the spring when the roads are clear and deliver it to a printer there, but he is a long way off from that. He has amassed a very great, and very odd, collection of stories. Some are his own experiences; some tell of our remarkable sea deliverances, our journey here under providential guidance. He also has an account of the miraculous founding of the town itself, as told by Reverend Johnson and the original settlers. The rest is a rag and tag collection of signs and portents, dreams and miracles, collected from goodness knows where. Strange lights, comets burning across the skies, houses riven with strange hauntings and noise from invisible drummer boys, women and beasts who bear monstrous progeny, conjurors' books that refuse to burn, and I do not know what else. I do not know who is gulling him, but he has more old wives' tales here than any village crone keeps in her noddle.

As I write, Elias paces the room, cracking his long fingers to ease the red knotted joints. As he walks, he talks, and as he talks his pale eyes gleam with a cold fanatical fire, every bit as wintry as the sun striking the ice outside.

"Winter grips harder. Ships freeze in Boston harbor. The wolves grow ever bolder. Children sicken. Cattle die."

"But that happens every year."

"This year is worse, next will be worse still, and so on, until it snows year round. This year is 1660. We enter the Last Days, Mary. We have scant years left until 1666, the Year of the Beast. Can't you understand? Satan's reign is all about us. We must be ever vigilant lest we be corrupted along with the rest. Only the pure, the untainted, will be fit to welcome back the coming Christ."

Sometimes he comes very near, leaning to see what I write. This close attention has me squirming. I smell his fishy breath, feel it on my cheek and neck, and struggle not to choke and gag.

He truly believes in Christ's Coming, and that His kingdom will have Beulah at its center. His only worry is that this will happen before he can get his pamphlet to the printers. I think him more than a little mad.

## 73

*Hunger stalks the town* and the wolves do grow bolder, he is right about that. There was fresh snow last night, and this morning Tobias showed me a set of tracks going straight down the main street. Broad fore-foot, narrow hind.

"Perhaps it is a dog."

"That's no dog."

His friend Ned spat. It is so cold his spittle froze before it hit the snow. The tracks went as far as the Meeting House. They stopped beneath the line of heads, as though it scented its own kind nailed up there, then went on. By the door the snow was melted, frozen yellow where she had squatted.

"Shows what her thinks of yon." Ned grinned, his already discolored teeth streaked and rimmed red with blood from his bleeding gums.


74.

*Goody Johnson's eldest girls* have fallen sick now, so I often spend the day with her, helping her with the smaller children, just as Rebekah helps Sarah. I do not feel like a servant. Goody Johnson is nearing her time and is great with child, so she needs all the help that I can offer. Besides, she has been kind to us.

If it were not for her, we would be like to use our seed corn for eating or starve. If we share what she gives among us, we might just get by. When the work is done and the children quiet in their corner, we sit in the kitchen, and she gives me warm spiced ale with cake to dip in it. She has asked me of my past. I have told her what I can, but she knew I was keeping something back.

A silence brooded between us, rendering some moments stilted and awkward until one day she asked me.

"You have not told me all, have you, Mary?"

I cannot lie to her. She is so good, so gentle, to lie would be sinful.

"Don't ask me."

I cannot speak of it, not in this house.

I hear his words again: "I am His representative."

*"Thou shalt not suffer a witch to live."* I have heard him thunder it from the pulpit.

"I think I guess at it. I was not always as I am now." Her faded eyes looked deep into mine and seemed to take on darker blue and violet. "When I was your age I ran wild. I too lived with my grandmother. I never knew my father; he was a soldier. My mother left to follow him, and no one ever saw her again. I reached womanhood in a country plunging into war. Many parts became beyond the law, and into this breach stepped men bent on malice, intent on fishing in waters already

199

troubled and muddy. I think you know the kind of whom I speak. They came to our town, to root out witchcraft, so they said, but their real interest was in their fee, twenty shillings to free the town from witches. My grandmother was dead by then, thank the Lord she was spared, but their attention turned to me instead."

As she spoke, my own memories flooded me, causing my blood to heat and freeze me, hot with hatred, cold with fear.

"They hunted me down like an animal, bound me and threw me into the millpond to see if I would float. I sank. I was bound hand and foot; I could not reach the surface, and even if I did, I would be hanged for a witch. I was drowning. I was on the bottom looking up at them. I can still see their faces through the rippling water, encircled above me, waiting for it to happen.

"Then suddenly the surface of the water broke with a great splash. Someone was swimming down to me. Strong arms went round me, pulling me to the surface. He was a young preacher, on his way to his first parish. He had followed the hue and cry, and when he saw what they had done, he dived in to bring me back for God. He denounced the Witchfinder and his men as charlatans, interested in money, not saving souls. He cast the demons from me, right there and then. Along with a deal of water from my insides." She smiled at the memory, and then her lips gave a bitter little twist, as if life had failed to give her the joy and hope that moment had promised. "He baptized me that day, there in the millpond, and a good few others besides. And when he left, I went with him."

"He saved you?"

"That's right. I owe him my life. I vowed to make him a good wife and lead a pious life. And I have. I have bowed my head in prayer and obedience, I have borne his children." She clutched my hands. "I changed. You can do the same!"

"What if I can't?" The words came out in a whisper.

She looked away and withdrew her hands.

"Then the Lord have mercy upon you."

"I will try, Goody Johnson. I truly will."

I said what she wanted to hear, because she had been kind and I wanted to please her. I could not say what I really felt: If I had to choose between the life she'd had and death by drowning, I would choose the latter.

75.

*I have seen the wolf.* I was on the edge of the wood, looking for nuts that the squirrels might have missed; some have lost their virtue and do not have much taste, but they can be ground with acorns to be made into flour, and the butternuts are as good as ever they were. I was clearing snow and scratching about when I felt my skin begin to prick. I looked up expecting to see Jaybird and wondering what he was doing here, when there she was, not ten yards off. Very like a dog but bigger, with grayish, dun-colored fur, pale tipped at the neck where it thickened in a shaggy ruff, and a black stripe running down the back. She stood on broad forelegs, big about the shoulders and chest. Her flanks were thinner, moving in and out with her breathing, her body tapering back to slender hind legs and narrow hindquarters. She was panting, her breath puffing white into the cold air, her red tongue lolling through her long white teeth. Her eyes were golden. She watched me and I watched her.

I was not afraid. I just willed her to go away. Hunger caved her belly, and I know they bait traps for her at the edge of the forest.

We both stood quite still, caught in a gap of time, then she wheeled away, as though she heard my message, bounding off, her dark shape lost in the crowded blackness of trees.

## 76.  February 1660

Goody Johnson is dead.
She died last week, the second week in February. She died in childbirth.

"She should never be having another. This 'un could kill her," Martha had said all along, and said so again as she hurried to the birthing room, then looked over her shoulder lest she had been overheard. Her words could be taken as ill-wishing, and a midwife must be careful.

Martha and I went together for the birthing. Goody Johnson labored long, to the brink of exhaustion and beyond. It took through one day and into the next. Goody Johnson was narrow, despite having had so many children, and had no strength to push anymore. The baby was big, and when he came the cord was twisted about his neck. I had to fairly pull him from her. I cut the cord and gave him to Martha, who took one look and covered him with a cloth.

She stared at the mother, who lay as though dead, and turned away, her own face gray and drawn.

"I fear that they will be buried together."

Martha tried everything she knew, but she could not save her. She had given the last of her strength and was just drifting away from us. She woke once and asked to see the babe. Martha replied with a little shake of her head. She turned her face to the wall, eyes closed, lids deep violet against her sallow skin.

She never opened them again.

Martha called for Reverend Johnson. He was reluctant to enter the chamber, smelling as it did of blood and birthing. He held to the Bible teaching that a woman is unclean after giving birth.

"If you want to see her in this life, you better come now," Martha said to him. "And bring your children that they may say farewell to their mother and their brother."

Goody Johnson lay still, as though she had already begun her last and most perilous journey, but the sound of her children's voices and their tears seemed to bring her back. Her eyelids flickered, and her thin hand stirred on the counterpane. The Reverend Johnson's voice rose in sonorous praise to the Lord. Martha and I withdrew, leaving the family to spend their last time together.

Outside it was snowing again. We began our trudge back.

"Another good woman gone." Martha sighed as we trod through the snow. She looked tired, defeated. Every year of her age showed in her face. "Ours is a hard calling. Birth and death go together too often for my liking. Let us hope we don't get the blame for it."

She said no more, but I knew her meaning. To be a midwife, to be a healer, brings danger. If everything goes well, then all are grateful, but when things go wrong, as they do often enough, well, that is a different matter. Those that heal can harm, that's what they whisper; those that cure can kill.

We walked past the Meeting House. Another wolf has been caught, its freshly severed head dripping blood onto the drifting snow. The bared teeth snarl defiance and the eyes, glazed in death, still glow yellow. I hope it is not the one that I saw at the edge of the forest, but there is no way to tell.

## 77.  Early March 1660

*The ground is hard as iron.* Despite what the calendar says, winter seems reluctant to loosen its grip. Goody Johnson has lain a fortnight, and still her grave is not dug.

She and the child lie wrapped in the same winding-sheet, lodged in an outbuilding, where the cold will keep them from corruption until the earth is thawed enough to take a spade.

## 78.  March 1660

*Goody Johnson was buried today.* Elias Cornwell conducted the service. Reverend Johnson stood, head bowed, surrounded by tearful older children and sobbing little ones.

"Man that is born of woman . . ."

The words rang out over the snow-patched hill as Goody Johnson was lowered into the pit. It was bitterly cold. The Reverend Johnson wiped at his nose and dabbed at his eyes, although whether he cried from the wind or in sorrow, who can tell?

## 79. Late March 1660

This Sunday Reverend Johnson took St. Paul as the text of his Sunday sermon.

"It is better to marry than to burn."

Few in front of him mistake his meaning. Reverend Johnson is casting about for a new wife before the grass on the grave of the old one has grown to a finger width. He wants someone to care for his brood of children and warm his bed, he makes no secret of it. There is no lack of candidates. Girls and their mothers scrape what they have left in their larders into bread, cakes, and pies for him. He is invited to different houses every night for supper.

Deborah Vane, for one, has set her cap at him. She no longer fidgets and yawns her way through Sunday service. She no longer needs to be prodded awake. She now sits upright, back straight, eager eyed, hanging on every word that issues from the pulpit, hardly taking her eyes off Reverend Johnson except to make notes in a little book she keeps on her lap, unless it is Elias

Cornwell's turn to preach. Then she falls to giggling with her sister, whispering comments about him behind her hand, as she did before.

Across the aisle from her, Ned Cardwell sits, neck and ears red, studying his boots. He is a hired man, but he has ambitions and has made no secret of his admiration for Deborah. Along the row from him, Josiah Crompton is also down in the mouth. He had hopes too, or so Tobias tells me. Deborah ignores both of them. She only has eyes for the Reverend Johnson.

## 80. March–April 1660

The Reverend Johnson does not have eyes for her. In the ordinary way of things, I would be pleased. I like Deborah about as much as she likes me, but I find no pleasure in Deborah's humiliation. I wish that Reverend Johnson would marry her, as quickly as may be. That would be far, far better than what has happened now.

The preacher has turned his eyes to Rebekah. Even though he knows that she is promised to Tobias, he has been to her father, asking for her hand.

I found Rebekah crying, which is hardly surprising. I'd cry too, and bitterly, if I was in her shoes.

"What does your mother think?"

"She's with me."

"Has your father given his answer?"

"Not yet."

"Then go to him. Plead with him. He'll not go against your happiness."

I pulled at her arm, trying to get her to her feet, but she slumped back, head on her arms, racked by fresh sobs.

"Come, Rebekah. It is not as bad as that—"

"It is worse."

"Worse?"

I did not understand. What could be worse than having to marry Reverend Johnson?

She looked up impatiently, her normally pale face red and puffed from so much crying.

"Do you not understand? Do I have to spell it out? I am with child!"

I sank down next to her.

"With child?"

"Yes," she hissed at me. "Speak softly and don't repeat everything I say."

"How?"

"How do you think?"

"Tobias?"

"Of course him." She twisted her soaked kerchief. "We thought to marry in the spring. Now this . . ." Her lips were trembling again.

"What about Martha? She will know ways . . ."

She grabbed me, digging her fingers into my arm.

"You are to say nothing to her! It would be a deadly sin, and besides it is Tobias's child!"

"Does he know?"

"Not yet."

"You must tell him. Now. He must go to your father and ask his permission to marry you straightaway."

"What if my father will not give it?"

"Then you must tell him the reason."

Her hazel eyes grew wide. "I cannot!"

"You must! With things at such a pass, there's no help for it! He will give his permission; the shame would be too great else. He would not want you to be known as unchaste . . ."

"Neither would I!" Her face reddened further. "I am not! And I do not want my father to think that of me."

"Go to your mother, then. Tell her. But do it quickly before your father has time to make up his mind in favor of Reverend Johnson."


## 81. April 1660

*The ground has softened* enough to take a plow. John Rivers is out all day, hacking at the land as if it were an enemy, driving his bullock team as if he would plow the whole village under. He begins at dawn, returning at dusk and speaking to nobody, his black brows lowering, his jaw set as if carved from granite.

Martha was not slow to guess the state of affairs when Sarah asked her if Rebekah had been to her for advice. Martha offered the help she could give, but this is refused again.

The two women sit muttering together by the fire, and I am not invited to join their counsel. I go to Rebekah, who keeps to her room, where she cries and sighs, waiting for her father's decision.

Tobias keeps out of the way. When he does appear Jonah and Martha shake their heads at him, and he walks as if on eggshells. He spends most of his time hiding in the byre with the animals or out in the forest.

We all wait to see what John Rivers will do. His answer is not long in coming. He loves his daughter, and liked Tobias well enough until this came to pass. He is not a man to go against his wife, and after much pleading from her, he gives his consent.

By Sunday the banns for Rebekah and Tobias will flutter on the door of the Meeting House, and by the end of the month they will be married.

# 82.

Reverend Johnson caught me after Sunday service as I was reading the banns on the Meeting House door.

"I want to speak with you," he said.

"Me, sir? What about?"

He did not reply; perhaps he thought my question too insolent. His dark eyes pierced into me. He gripped me by the chin, turning my face up to him.

"The foul fiend oft times hides behind a fair visage; have you not heard that, Mary?"

I could not say, his question having struck me dumb with terror. I shook my head as vigorously as I could, held as I was by his restricting fingers.

He seemed not to expect an answer.

"I have heard it. Aye, and seen it too." He let go of my chin. "I think you meddle in things that do not concern you."

"I? Meddle? I do not understand you."

"I think you do."

He said nothing more, just stood, hands clasped, staring at the notice of marriage.

Master Tobias Morse to Miss Rebekah Rivers . . .

I looked away hastily, not wanting to show that I understood him.

"If I've offended you, sir—"

"Do not seek to trick me with false servility." His deep voice was quiet but full of threat, just as the distant rumble of thunder promises a storm. "There is something about you that I do not trust. Elias thinks you harmless, but I might discover otherwise. I think he is ruled less by his mind than by other parts. Perhaps you lay a spell on him?"

"No, sir, I—"

"You come into my house," he went on, as if I had never spoken, as if to himself, "and my wife dies, my child besides. Perhaps you put a spell on them too?"

"Oh no, sir . . ."

The words dried in my mouth. The blood drained from my face. My breath came quick and small. I thought that I would faint. His accusations were so serious and set my mind in such a whirl that I could not think of anything at all.

"I look to find another and am straightway thwarted. How much ill luck can one man suffer before he looks to find a cause for it?"

"Cause, sir?"

"Witchcraft." He bent near, whispering the word into my ear, speaking so low and close that I wondered if I heard him aright. I felt his black eyes upon me, but I dared not look at him. I kept my eyes fixed on the ground. I do not know how it would have gone if one of his selectmen had not stepped up to speak with him.

"Go your ways, Mary," he said, dismissing me. "But I warn you. One breath more about you, and your days here are numbered."

I left with his warning ringing in my ears. I partly know why he is so displeased. He wanted Rebekah badly and rightly guesses that I would counsel my friend to follow her heart and use all my powers of persuasion to come between him and his hopes of her. He is a shrewd man, but his belief in spells and witchcraft warps his perceptions away from mere human sense into something else.

Our conversation was over in a minute. Sometimes I think I must have dreamed it. Other times I know that this is not so, that it really happened. The slightest recollection of any part of it makes me start awake in the night and begin to shake.

I will not tell Martha. It would worry the life out of her. I will endeavor to keep out of his way as much as possible and do nothing, *nothing*, to draw attention to myself.

83.

Winter has finally loosed its grip. A great rain has fallen, taking the remains of the snow with it. The sun warms, and everywhere there is the sound of running water. It is the time for plowing and planting. The deep rhythms of life abide even in this New World, with its savage beasts and great lowering forests, and its extremes of heat and cold.

Each day, great skeins of geese and duck fly over us, coming back from the south. I wonder about Jaybird and White Eagle. I have neither seen nor heard any sign of them. I worry about what Jaybird said about war and rumors of war. I wonder where they are and whether they will come back hereabouts, and if I will see them again.

Some of the plants they named for Jonah are bringing forth new shoots, and he has high hopes for the seeds I collected for him. The Physick Garden makes me sick for home. The little walled beds are set out in strict geometric shapes like the squire's knot garden, and the stands of sage and thyme give off a scent that reminds me so of my grandmother and the herbs she grew that I ache to see her again.

I had almost forgotten about the hare. I had not seen it or heard tell of it all winter long. Until yesterday evening.

I was down in the lower meadow. It is not far from the edge of the forest, and the light was fading, the night coming on. I was bringing the cows up for milking when suddenly a hare started up, right in front of me. I had no idea that it was even there, but they are cunning animals, hard to see in cover. They are also very shy and generally run from people, but this one did not. It looked at me, and its eyes were round and brown—a pair of human eyes in its tawny animal face. The broad nose twitched, drawing up the long split upper lip.

I know it is her, but why does she come? To warn, to watch over, to ask for vengeance? For a moment it seemed that she would speak to me, but from the direction of town came the sound of a dog barking and the hare leapt away, bounding off on its great back legs, zigzagging toward the line of trees.

## 84.

*Tobias and Rebekah are married.* I have gone back to Martha. Tobias has moved to the room I used to share with Rebekah. He has land of his own and will build a house for her there, but until that is finished, they will live with her mother and father, in the little room at the back of the house. Martha and I helped Sarah make it ready for them. The quilt looks splendid on the marriage bed.

In fact, the quilt was so admired by the folk who came to the wedding party that others have asked Martha to sew one for them. Martha thinks she could do well from this, particularly if I were to help her, but she has little cloth left and no means to make more. It must come from Salem.

The town shuns contact with the outside world, and the spring thaw has mired what roads there are, but as soon as it is possible to travel, Tobias plans to take a wagon to the market in Salem. He has been busy all winter, making tables, chairs, barrel staves. He will trade these for cloth, nails, seed, locks, hinges, things that we need and cannot be made. He will bring these back to sell. He has always worked hard, but now he works harder. He is full of schemes and ways to make money. He is determined to make a good life for Rebekah and the baby.

## 85. May Day Eve 1660

*Not everyone is happy* that Rebekah and Tobias are married. This Sunday the Reverend Johnson frowned from the pulpit, and his sermon was grimmer than ever. Deborah Vane shares his wrath. Her spleen spreads to her sister, Hannah, and their friends Sarah Garner and Elizabeth Denning. They narrow their eyes at us in church and turn to whisper to each other whenever they see Rebekah and me together. I thought them harmless, mere irritations, like mosquitoes in summer, until I met them one morning coming from the forest. They have baskets filled with flowers that grow here. The woods now are garnished with green and the floor carpeted with color. Their baskets spill spring flowers: spikes of blossom, sprigs of lobelia, delicate pink roses, orchids, and lilies. But beneath I glimpse plants of a different kind: the purple heads of monkshood, something like hemlock, and the cowled head and single thrusting tongue of what looks like a kind of wild arum.

"Where do you go to? The forest?" Deborah asked, feigning innocence while the others sniggered.

"Aye." I had my own basket and trowel. "I am going to meet Jonah. We are to collect plants together. He says the garden wants color."

At this, the sniggering turned to outright laughter.

"You do not go to the forest to collect *flowers.*" Sarah Garner sneered down at me.

"And you do not go with Master Morse," Elizabeth Denning added.

"Do I not? What do I do there, then?"

"We know." Deborah looked at the others, who simpered together, their eyes sly.

"*We* know," they repeated together.

"Oh. And what do you know?"

"That that is not all that you do." Deborah leaned toward me, whispering, her hand guarding her mouth in a gesture of exaggerated secrecy. "We know!"

"Know what?"

"That you talk to the animals. Bend trees to your

will. Conjure spirits. Meet with the Indians. Dance naked!" She hissed the last, and then brayed with laughter. "See! She blushes!"

The others joined in, hooting their glee at my expense.

"Who would not!" I felt myself going hot. "Such a suggestion is immodest!"

"You blush from guilt. We know what you do." Deborah stressed each word, jabbing a finger at me. "You put spells on people. Don't worry." She looked at the others. "We will not tell. Not if you promise to help us."

"Help you? In what way?" I tried to keep my voice steady, but the sweat was breaking over my body. Everything they said filled me with fear.

"Don't pretend innocence. We know what you can do. Today is May Day Eve—a very great night for witches, I believe." Her eyes grew sly again. "A night when you can see things."

"Like your future husband," Hannah supplied. "And bind him to you, if you have the skill!" She all but squealed the last, her weasel features screwed up with excitement. "That's where you can help us."

"I cannot. I do not have the skill you speak of."

"We know that you do." Deborah smiled. "You did it for Rebekah; you can do it for us."

"What?"

"Rebekah and Tobias. You wove a spell to bind him to her. A love spell." The others giggled. "That was your work."

"There is certainly magic there." I tried to laugh. "But it is not of my making."

"Do not try to hoodwink us. You secured Tobias for her. He would not have chosen her; why would he? She is ugly. You even turned the Reverend Johnson to her and away from me!" Her eyes narrowed. "Or perhaps you want him for yourself!"

"Me and Reverend Johnson!" I had to laugh at that. "Now I know you are dreaming!"

"Elias Cornwell, then!" Sarah Garner burst out. "Everyone knows he won't hear a word against you and favors you above all others!"

"That may be so." There was no point in denying it. Reverend Cornwell *did* single me out. His interest in me has continued long after he could scribe for himself. "But I have done nothing to encourage him."

"Yes, you have!" Deborah Vane hissed.

I shook my head. The truth was opposite. I tried to avoid him as much as possible. His attention was like some lanky weed, the more you slash at it, the more it grows.

"I have not! You are mad. All of you . . ."

So that's the way of it. Sarah Garner wants Elias Cornwell for herself. She is tall and plain, with a long thin face. She would make a good wife for him, but I will not help her, nor the others either. They have it all planned out. Deborah wants the Reverend Johnson, Elizabeth Denning wants Josiah Crompton. And they want me to cast spells to secure these men as husbands for them.

"What about you?" I chucked Hannah under her pointed little chin. "Are you not too young to choose a sweetheart?"

I smiled, still trying to make light of it. She can't be much more than nine or ten.

"I'm not too young." She smiled back, showing her little splintery needle teeth. "I want Tobias." She lisped the end of his name. "I want you to put a curse on Rebekah. Make a poppet. Stick pins in it."

"Rebekah is my friend." My grip tightened on her chin. "And if you do anything, anything to harm her or her child—"

"Stop it!" She struggled away from me. "Deborah, she's hurting!"

"I'll do more than that if you're not careful." I looked at all of them. "I will not help you. And my advice is to leave well alone."

They went on, their baskets full of flowers for May garlands, although such things are forbidden here. I then turned homeward, trying to dismiss their words as girlish spite and mischief-making, but still I found much on which to ponder. The herbs that lay under the blossom, that lay in the bottom of the baskets, those were herbs for a witch's brewing. I know, from my grandmother, that there is black as well as white, dark as well as light, but for all she stood accused of, she ever followed the right-hand path. She would never have used her skills for evil or for frivolous purposes. I can guess at what those girls intend, and it chills me. They have no skill, I'm sure of that. All they have to sustain them is natural malice, yet somehow they have contrived to turn tables on me, taking power from me. I feel it draining, turning my blood to ice water, leaving my heart weighted inside me as cold and heavy as stone.

## 86. May 1660

"*Signs of witchcraft*, of hideous practice, have been found in the forest!"

The Reverend Johnson's voice thunders from the pulpit. All talking is forbidden, but alarm rustles through the congregation like leaves stirring in the wind. I look along the rows. Deborah Vane has gone quite white, as has her sister next to her. Sarah Garner and Elizabeth Denning study their shoes. There have been rumors all week of this. Traces of a fire found in a forest clearing. Ashes on the ground, what looks like tallow, and a strewing of some evil brew, fetid herbs as well as some frogs boiled to whiteness.

"Satan's work. Here at Beulah. Profanity! Iniquity! I warn you, my people, we must be ever vigilant! Ever watchful. The foul fiend and his minions are all around us—even at Beulah! They caper and gibber in the forest, carrying on their heathen rites not a mile from God's house!"

He is talking about the Indians. He goes on, warming to his theme, warning that they are everywhere, living all through the forest, as common as fleas in a dog's pelt. That we do not see them makes them all the more dangerous. They are the Devil's instruments, in league with the Evil One himself, intent on driving us from our rightful place in this land. He orders patrols to guard the settlement, men with muskets to go through the woods.

I see the girls draw breath again. They sit back, eyes closed in silent prayers of thanks. Hannah smirks at her sister and starts to play with a doll she keeps on her lap.

## 87

*I have been listening* for Jaybird, trying to distinguish one cry from another, waiting for his call to sound out from the birds' empty clamor. This evening I thought I heard it, measured, insistent, close to the house.

As much as I want to see him, I have been forbidden the woods by Martha, but I wait until she goes next door to Sarah. I must go to him and warn him. I cannot let him walk into danger. The fear is great here. The patrols continue. If he is found anywhere near, he or his grandfather, he will be shot.

He is just in the edge of the forest, a little way from the house. I am glad to see him, and he has a gift for me, a pair of beaded moccasins such as he wears in the forest. But I have little chance to thank him or to do anything more than warn him. Almost as soon as we meet I hear Martha calling. I hide the moccasins inside my shawl and hope to sneak past Martha, but she catches me. She is all of a bother, her rosy face white and mottled. Jonah is away, helping Tobias with the house he is building for Rebekah. We are alone together.

"What are you doing out alone in the woods?"

"Nothing. Walking merely."

"You know I have forbidden you! You know the talk there's been about you! Now especially—"

"Aye, and I have obeyed you. Except for tonight. There was something I had to do."

"You do not go to conjure?" There is no one else here, but Martha spoke low, as if the very walls could betray us. She does not believe that what was found in the forest has anything to do with Indians.

"Hush, Martha! That was not me. You know I would do nothing so stupid!"

"I did not think that you did. Yet you would keep this!"

She holds out my Journal.

"Where did you find it?"

"In your box."

I snatch, but she holds tighter. The first page tears between us.

I hold the line curled in my fist.

*I am Mary. I am*

"*A witch!*" Martha hisses, white to the lips. "You are mad to write it! If I can find it, so can they. You could get us all hanged!"

"You knew I kept it."

"But not what you wrote! I never sought to pry before, Mary. It is not my way. I thought you wrote as other girls would, of everyday things, lovers and dreams. I should have known!" She holds the page hard, creasing it. "You are not as other girls, are you?"

She makes a dash to throw the papers on the fire, but I am quicker. Words have power. These are mine. She has no right to destroy them. I stop her before she reaches the hearth.

"No, Martha. You cannot do this."

The will seeps out of her. Her hands lower.

"Then you do it."

"I will, I promise."

"Do it now. It will not be long before suspicion turns away from Indians and will-o'-the-wisps, things that do not exist. There will be searches. They will come looking for evidence. Poppets, spells, curses, tablets. If I can find this, so can they. And if they do, no power on earth can save you." She brandished the papers, waving them in my face and throwing them down on the table before me. "Burn it! Get rid of it!"

With that she retired, leaving me alone. I went to my little room at the back of the house and dragged my box out from under my bed. The box and its contents reminded me of my mother. Even as I opened it, I seemed to breathe her scent: attar of rose, spiced with the clove of gillyflower. At the top of the box is the quilt Martha and I are making. Under that is my pouch.

I took the slip of paper still curled in my hand, and folding it small, put it in the pouch with my little stock of coin, the locket my grandmother gave me, my mother's ring, the half a silver shilling that was Jack's gift to me. I tucked the beaded moccasins down toward the bottom of my box and went back to the main room, fully intending to do what Martha expected, but I felt lonely, bereft. For all I love her, Martha is not my mother.

Burn it? Why should I? No one would think of forcing Elias Cornwell to consign the nonsense he writes to the fire. Unbidden my thoughts turned back to my mother. She gave me ink and paper, and I have used it to good effect. She is not like Martha, not afraid of her own shadow. She would not countenance such a craven act. For all she is an ocean away and I only knew her but for one day, I feel her presence suddenly. *Do not doubt that I love you*—that is what her letter said. I did not want to believe her words when I first read them, but I have changed my opinion. Many are separated, not least by death, and do not cease to love each other. I think that she did love me and loves me still.

I sat in the chair for a long time, watching the red heart of the fire crumble to ash.

I was roused by noises above my head. I started, thinking Martha would come down to find that I had not done as she said. There was no further movement, no feet on the ladder, she must have just been turning over in her bed. I relaxed, but my eyes stayed on the ceiling, caught by the quilt frame slung up there. My mother gave me something else—the cloth we are using to make the quilt.

I know what I will do.

## 88.

*I started that very night*, folding the pages thin as spills, tucking them into the padding that goes between the cover and the backing. They may search all they like, they will not find it now.

## 89.  June 1660

*The days stretch* to midsummer, staying light late into the night. When the day's work is done, Tobias and Jonah pack a supper and make their way to Tobias's plot. They take advantage of the light nights to clear the land and work on the house. Sometimes John Rivers goes with them. Sarah and Rebekah sit out with Martha and me to stitch my quilt.

It is made from the cloth my mother gave me and a fine piece of linsey-woolsey that Tobias brought me back from Salem. The color is a deep midnight blue, and I sketch my own designs upon it: flowers for my grandmother's garden, sails for the ships that brought us here, pine trees and oak leaves for the forest, feathers for the people who live in it, little cabins for us.

Martha frowns and clucks; such designs are not traditional. But the quilt is mine, and I care not a fig what she thinks. She can put her spirals in the corners and border it with an unending vine. I want my patterns left alone. I design them wide, to act like pockets. Later, I work like Penelope, undoing the stitches of the day, slotting each page away.

90.

*I left off sewing* because Sarah arrived here all of a state. Joshua Rivers has gone missing. Sarah thought him abed with the other little ones, but somehow he managed to sneak out while she was at a neighbor's and Rebekah was milking. She did not notice until just before retiring, when she did her final rounds. She thinks that he might have followed the men to where they are building Tobias's house. They took Joseph with them but said Joshua was too young. He is scarce turned seven, and little, but stout of heart and strong of will. He was exceeding angry to be left out, and vented his spleen on woodwork and livestock, so much so he was sent early to bed.

Martha and I tried our best to soothe her, reasoning that if he followed, he surely will have found them and will be back with the men in the morning. What else can we say?

The men returned without him. All day they have been searching. The whole town has been out.

Nigh about evening, just as the sun was setting, Martha came to me with a request. She wanted me to scry for him, to use the power of Seeing, to find him. At first I was not sure that I had heard her aright.

"You ask this of me? After all that you said? I could put us all in danger; those were your very words."

"Only if folk find out. You can do it, Mary. I know you have the Sight. They have searched high and low, and night draws on. What with wild beasts and Indians—"

"They would not hurt him."

"How do you know? I've heard tell they take children for their own."

I shook my head. "If they find him, they will bring him home." I half thought of going to Jaybird to ask his help, but I have no way of knowing where he is now.

She regarded me steadily.

"What if I cannot?"

I knew the way of it from watching my grandmother, but it is not a thing that can be taught, you have to be born with it.

"I know you can. At least you must try."

Still I hesitated. Divining like this had not always been seen as witchcraft. Old Queen Elizabeth had her soothsayers, so my grandmother said, and in the old days even the squire's wife had come to my grandmother asking her to find something lost. Times change, however. To try it in this place, at this time, could be an act of the utmost folly.

"What will I use as a pan?"

"I will go to Sarah, beg her big pewter bowl—"

"No. She will wonder what you want with it, at this time especially." I pointed to the tub kept by the hearth. "That will do." The tub was fashioned from a solid tree trunk and was brimful with fresh water. I had filled it myself. "Bar the door. Let no one enter. If I am caught . . ."

I did not have to say what would happen. I drew up a stool and stared down into the water. At first, I could see nothing but my own reflection and through that, the wood streaked and grooved with marks made by the awl. The surface settled until it was absolutely still. I could see tiny specks of dust floating on it. Then it began to shudder, tiny ripples running to the edges as if the vessel was shaken from beneath. The water became black. I could no longer see through it, and green vegetation crept from the margins. It looked like the swamp. I seemed to see broken stumps of trees breaking dark water. Two trees had fallen against each other, forming a bridge to an island, a mere clump of vegetation. Suddenly I could see him. I gripped hard on to the sides of the tub, my breath coming fast. He was in the middle of the islet, huddled against a rotten tree stump. His face was pale, dirt-streaked and tear-stained, but he was alive. I could see his chest rising and falling. Then the vision went, and I could see my own face, white and strained, my eyes black, staring back.

"He's in the swamp."

"Mercy!" Martha's hand flew to her mouth. "How ever did he get there?"

"He must have lost his way in the darkness and wandered deeper and deeper, unable to find the path out."

The swamp was some distance from the settlement. A dark, dismal place of broken trees and open water surrounded by quaking bog and quivering ground that might take the weight of a boy who was light, like Joshua. Any man would sink hip-deep or further. It was a miracle Joshua was not already drowned.

"That is where he is." I looked back into the barrel, conjuring the vision again in my memory. "There is a tall pine next to a stand of cedars. He is northeast from there. I can tell by the angle of the setting sun striking his face. But how will you tell them where to search?"

"I will think of something. Bless you, Mary. You did good work this day."

I shook the barrel, making the water tremble, destroying the image for good. "Let us wait. We will give thanks when he is home safely."

Martha hurried to find Jonah. The search was already widening toward the swamp, and it proved to be a simple task to nudge the searchers in the right direction. No one suspects anything, and Joshua has been brought back safe and sound. Some advised a good whipping, but John Rivers is a kind man, and so glad to see his son that all he gave him was a severe scolding, a night in the open being punishment enough. Joshua is confined to the house and garden and gets under our feet more than somewhat.


91.

*Midsummer's Day.* As hot as any I've known, although no sun shone. The clouds hung thick and low over the town from early morning. It was oppressive, like stifling under a hot wet blanket. Dusk came early to a loud chorus of crickets and frogs. Suddenly that stopped and night came on, as dark as winter.

There was little light to work, and the quilt felt damp, soaking up moisture from the atmosphere. At Martha's suggestion, we went inside and lit the candles. She felt as though a storm was coming, and as if to prove her right, little flickers of light showed on the horizon to the south. As yet far off, but it was enough to get the quilt packed up.

With Rebekah in her fifth month, Tobias was away

that night, clearing his acres and working on their house. Jonah went with him, together with John Rivers and Joseph, leaving us women alone at home. We went to Sarah's house, and Rebekah asked me to stay with her for company. Good that she did. Martha stayed too. She does not like the thunder and did not want to be alone in the coming storm.

We went to sleep expecting it, but we woke thinking that the world was truly coming to an end. I do not share Martha's fear of storms, but this was the most ferocious that I have ever known. Rebekah and I clutched each other as fearsome flashes lit the room white and blue. Thunder followed in less than a heartbeat, each crack louder and more terrible than the one before. Rain came down with furious force, drumming on the roof and the sides of the house. Above us the little ones cried out. The ladder creaked as Sarah went to them, and their screams turned to whimpers of piteous fear.

Suddenly, through the storm's rage, within the chaos of roaring sound, it was possible to hear a human voice raised in shrieking terror. But none was brave enough to see who it was or to risk a soaking to offer succor.

The next morning dawned clear, the rain gone, but the storm had done much damage. Roads and paths washed away. Crops in the fields well nigh flattened. All the petals battered from Martha's flowers.

It did not take us long to find who the night shrieker was: Tom Carter, the old man who lives near the forest in a hut little better than a hovel, making his living by brewing strong liquor from what he finds in the forest.

The night of the storm, he went out into the trees to relieve himself; this is what he said. Suddenly a bolt of lightning turned the blackness around him to day, and he saw them, the white shapes of spirits flitting through the woods, fleeing from tree to tree.

The sight had him running for town, shirt half out, clutching his breeches about him, shrieking as though all the devils in Hell were streaming along behind him.

Some were inclined to laugh, especially those who saw him, and blame it on drinking his own stock, but others took a different view.

Apparitions and violent storms are to be taken seriously. Tom Carter was taken to tell his story to Reverend Johnson and Elias Cornwell. They took the still terrified Tom back to the forest, together with Jethro Vane, Nathaniel Clench, and Ezekiel Francis, who are selectmen and town constables, and other members of the watch.

They have found something. The rumor spreads round the town faster than fire through stubble, but nobody knows just what.

$\mathcal{J}$ust after noon, there was a hammering on the door. Martha opened it to find Jethro Vane and Ezekiel Francis standing there with another of the constables.

"You two are to come with us."

"What for?" Martha looked Francis in the eye. "Tell me, brother-in-law."

"Reverend's orders." Ezekiel colored like a turkey cock.

"Are we arrested?"

"No. But—"

Not yet, his eyes seemed to say.

"Go your ways, then. I've got work to do. Hungry men to feed. Some haven't got time to swan round the village bullying folk. They are out in the fields and expected directly."

"It's Reverend's orders."

"If the Reverend Johnson has business, he can come here to me."

Jethro Vane made a move toward her, as if to take her by force, but the other two men held back. They looked at each other, quandary plain on their faces. This was not expected. They did not know what to do.

Finally Ezekiel Francis said, "We'll be back."

They went, leaving Martha all in a heap. She took

a moment to recover herself, then she told me, "Go and get Sarah. When they come back, we must all be together. Our hopes can't rest on the men. They won't be back till evening, never mind what I told him."

They came in a bunch, turning the house into a court, Reverend Johnson and Nathaniel Clench with them. Nathaniel Clench is magistrate, there to ensure justice and fairness, but everyone knows he's Johnson's man.

"Where were you last night, the night of the storm?" Reverend Johnson did the questioning.

"In bed, asleep," Martha answered.

"Not you, Martha." He turned to me. "You."

"In bed asleep. The same as her."

"You did not leave the house?"

"No."

His eyebrows rose. Before he could disbelieve me, Sarah spoke.

"She was with us. Our men are away so we stayed together. Mary slept with Rebekah beside her."

Johnson had not expected this intervention. He looked at Sarah, snarling impatience, like an animal cheated of prey.

"We were all together," she insisted, her voice calm and quiet.

Rebekah and Martha nodded to confirm what she said.

He turned to Rebekah.

"And you did not leave? Either separately"—he paused, a smile forming; his voice dropped until it was almost purring—"or together?"

We shook our heads.

"Why do you question us?" Sarah asked. She was addressing Reverend Johnson, but her eyes blazed at the other men. Nathaniel Clench is brother-in-law to her. He dropped his eyes and stared at the floor.

"I do not question you," Reverend Johnson answered. "I question them. There has been a gathering in the woods. We found evidence."

"A gathering? For what purpose?"

"To conjure spirits, woman!" Ezekiel Francis spoke up. "You must have heard about Tom Carter. He is a witness."

"Of what?" Sarah sneered her contempt. "His own drunken imaginings."

"We have evidence of more than one female presence." Reverend Johnson looked at Rebekah and me. "Do you recognize these things?"

"My daughter is with child!" Sarah stepped forward, thoroughly riled now. "Do you think she would risk that unborn life to cavort in the woods at night?" She shook her head. "No. You must look elsewhere."

"Perhaps they left without your noticing." Ezekiel's squinted eyes closed further.

"There's only one door in our house. They would have had to clamber over me to get to it. Or do you suggest *I* joined them?" Her tone could have frozen water. "That is the way such questions lead, is it not?"

She fixed the men with her icy stare. Her brother-in-law, Nathaniel Clench, looked even more uncomfortable. Some of the others with him. Martha and I were easy game, but Sarah Rivers was a different matter. She was well-connected, she and John highly respected.

"We suggest nothing of the kind." Johnson noticed Clench's reaction and stirrings among the other men and gestured for Francis to be quiet. "It still remains the case that these things were found and that they are female garments."

I stepped forward to inspect them. A cap and a petticoat. Both much creased and trampled with forest dirt and still damp from the night before.

"These would fit neither of us. The petticoat is too large for me but too small for Rebekah. The cap is too small for either."

The cap was so tiny that it could have belonged to a child. The hem of the petticoat was decorated with open embroidery work.

"Why come to us? You must find a girl little bigger than a child, and one who wears vanities under her clothing."

I looked at Jethro Vane. The description fitted his nieces, not us, and he knew it.

## 93

*Sarah was loud* in her indignation that suspicion should have fallen upon us, but Martha and I remained silent. We know how these things can go. She has spoken to John, who has advised caution. He thinks that there will be some simple explanation and then the whole thing will blow over like a summer storm.

## 94. July 1660

*Surely enough,* Deborah and Hannah Vane have been questioned, and surely enough, they have conjured a suitable tale between them. They had plenty of warning and time in which to do so.

Their story goes in this way. They were walking in the woods, days since, and were suddenly so overcome by heat that they had to remove some of their clothing and, oh yes, it was a petticoat and it was a cap. They walked on, still much fatigued, and in a moment of forgetfulness they neglected to bring said garments from the forest.

They are believed. Of course they are. They are the nieces of Jethro Vane, and he is a powerful man in the town. Suspicion flits by them, light as a butterfly. I wait with dread for it to land on me again.

I am not guilty. I have done nothing. I was safe abed. I have witnesses, but in these matters such things count for little, and innocence is no defense. The forces of the law already have beaten a path to my door. I try not to think of what could happen if they find more. I do not trust those girls. They are headstrong and foolish, and their natures are full to the brim with malice. If they are caught in any kind of meddling, they will seek to turn the guilt in a second. They will look about to cast the blame on someone else. That someone may be myself.

*witness*

## 95. July–August 1660

*I write this* as fast as can be and put it into the quilt. Write and stitch, write and stitch, far into the night.

The girls *were* out there on that night, conjuring spirits. I know it as sure as if I had been out there with them. The storm broke over them, causing them to stop whatever nonsense they were performing and run in panic. That's when Tom Carter saw them.

I thought that would stop them. But it did not.

They were nearly caught, and that should have been warning enough. What happened on Midsummer Night should have put an end to their madness. Instead they feed upon it. Now they believe they have the power to conjure storms. They lose flesh, their eyes burn. I know the witch's calendar. Each month, as the moon waxes to full, the girls' antic behavior increases. Hannah has been removed twice from Sunday service for interrupting sermons, talking loudly, then falling to giggling and laughing uncontrollably. What they do is like a sickness, a fever in the blood. They practice not just in the forest but in barns, in one another's houses. I have been keeping watch. I have seen the candle-flicker, the shadow of dancing figures, turning on the walls.

*The woods begin to color.* The fields ripen toward autumn, but the turning year has brought a series of afflictions: beasts dead for no reason, others giving milk that is thick and yellow and bloody in the pail, then a tremendous hailstorm that beat the crops down. It is as if a dismal black cloud has settled over the town, a sense of foreboding, as though something bad is about to happen.

Reverend Johnson has ordered a Day of Humiliation, of solemn prayer and fasting, a time for us to ask for God's forgiveness, for we have attracted His displeasure.

97.

*The Day of Humiliation.*
Reverend Johnson had barely started his sermon when there was a commotion. Hannah Vane pitched forward from her seat in a dead faint. Then Deborah went down beside her, and her cousin with her. The girls were falling off their benches like frozen starlings. Reverend Johnson stopped and ordered them taken out. They were carried, some rigid and unbending as timbers, others flopping and heavy so it took two men to bear them.

"The affliction has spread to the community, to the children. It is a very great wonder . . ."

Reverend Johnson spoke in a whisper, his face set in thunder, his eyes wide and deep with fear.

98.

*The girls are no better.* Some are struck dumb and lie as if dead, others rant and rave, tearing at themselves and their clothing, cursing and swearing at all who go near them. Pressured by Jethro Vane and others, Reverend Johnson has sent Elias Cornwell to Salem for help, for a doctor.

Meanwhile, rumors abound. Fragments of stories are passed from person to person. When pieced together, they begin to get near to the truth of what has happened.

I heard the official version of the tale from Martha, who had it from her sister Anne Francis, who, of course, knows everything. It goes this way: Deborah and Hannah Vane, Sarah Garner, Elizabeth Denning, and others unknown have been found dancing in a barn, shamefully unclad. They were discovered by a farmer who, hearing his beasts lowing, had gone to see what agitated them. He went armed with a musket, thinking that Indians might be stealing from him. He opened the door, expecting red men, and found girls instead, scrambling away, trying to hide their nakedness behind bales of hay.

Old Tom Carter had another version of the tale. This is what he told Jonah: It was not just any farmer. It was Jeremiah Vane himself who caught his own daughters and one of his nieces. He bid them get dressed, and in very great fear, he swore them to secrecy, making them promise to never do it again. All would have been well, and no one would ever have known about it. Except . . .

This is where the story gains salt and savor. I heard this from Rebekah, who got it from Tobias, who in turn had been told by Ned Cardwell.

Ned was in the loft spying on them. He had done this before, the dancing being a regular thing, according to him. Now, Ned is Jethro Vane's hired man, and Jethro Vane is a leader in the town and chief Selectman. He is also a bad master and a skinflint of some renown. He has ever treated Ned unkindly, and now Ned sees a way of getting back at him. He goes to the Vanes, Jethro and Jeremiah, demanding his freedom and the money to set up on his own. He wants Deborah as well, "if Jeremiah has a mind to it, or he'll go to the Reverend and tell how their daughters are using the family barns to prance about mother-naked and make free with Old Nick." The Vanes say they'll think on it. Ned tells Deborah they'd better think quick or the game is up.

Deborah must have told this to Hannah, who, since she is half crazed anyway, sought refuge in madness. The other girls followed her. All are mad now.

This is how I saw it, and so I said as much to Rebekah, as she failed to make sense of it.

Why pretend to be possessed? She cannot see the point of it. She cannot see how it makes them less guilty.

"Yes it does." I tried to explain. "If they are possessed by the Devil or some other spirit, then *they* are not responsible for what they do, the spirit is."

Rebekah looked at me curiously. "How do you know so much about it?"

I looked at her. She is older than me but seems younger, even though she is a woman now, and with child. She has put on flesh, her cheeks bloom. She is happy with Tobias; the house he is building is almost ready for her. I pray that this will not blight their lives together.

"Better that you don't know."

I turned away, trying to master my terror. The burden of guilt will not lie with the afflicted. They will look about to blame another, and I truly fear that it will be myself. These girls have ever hated me. Deborah particularly, and she is their leader. She has been riven by jealousy of Rebekah and is certain that I have thwarted her at every turn.

It can only be a matter of time before the finger of

accusation points to me. I know it as surely as I know that the sun will rise tomorrow and that the autumn leaves fall. My mind beats about like a bird in the attic, seeking escape this way and that. I've even thought of going to the Reverend Cornwell, throwing myself on his mercy, saying they come against me, asking for his protection. After all, he has paid me attention, and has made no secret of his admiration; but he would expect something in return, and then I remember Goody Johnson. I am truly between the anvil and the hammer. I could not bear to endure her same fate.

99.

A doctor came from Salem, brought by Elias Cornwell. He took one look at the girls and announced that no physick could cure this sickness. The madness was caused by witchcraft. He confirmed what Reverend Johnson had thought all along. The doctor was dismissed, and Nathaniel Clench has to find someone who can prove the presence of witchcraft.

It is a good thing my thoughts didn't run too long on going to Elias Cornwell. He was the first to take horse. There is a newcomer to the Colony, so he says, a man who has this kind of knowledge.

After him the other magistrates will come, and the judges. The statute is clear. If any man or woman be a witch, they shall be put to death.

According to Exodus 22:18: "Thou shalt not suffer a witch to live."

According to Leviticus 20:27: "A man also or woman that hath a familiar spirit, or that is a wizard, shall surely be put to death."

God's Law rules here.

## 100.  October 1660

*These are, perhaps, the last words* that I will ever write. Scribing them takes precious time, and I go in great fear of my life, but I feel that I must bear witness.

The man they have been awaiting has come.

Today was declared another Day of Humiliation. All were called to service in the Meeting House. There could be no exceptions. Absence would be seen as an admission of guilt.

The place was full. The afflicted girls were at the front. Some sat slumped, others lay on pallets. It had started with five girls: Deborah, Hannah, their cousin Judith Vane, Sarah Garner, and Elizabeth Denning. Now there were more. They had a whole bench to themselves. Hannah Vane sat at the end, mumbling to herself, twirling a poppet. She is allowed such things, being but a child. She is no child. As we took our places, she grabbed the doll about the middle, bunching the material, twisting viciously. Next to me Rebekah doubled, clutching her stomach. She gasped that her pains have started, the baby is coming early. I looked at Hannah, head rolling, tongue lolling. Her eyes gleamed malice, her sharp little teeth smiled at me, then she resumed her idiot dumb show.

Sarah and Martha helped Rebekah to rise. I went with them to take her outside. We found our way barred. Two tithing men stood before the door.

"None may leave. Orders of Reverend Johnson."

"Would you have her bear her child in the Meeting House?" Sarah's voice rang loud enough to reach our menfolk. Tobias and Jonah started up from their places, John Rivers with them.

The tithing men looked at each other. Neither is a man to go against orders.

Elias Cornwell appeared from nowhere.

"They may leave." His voice silky with feigned mercy. "Not you, Mary. You must stay." He whispered close. His fish breath in my ear, his thin hand forcing me back to my place. He nodded to the men behind me and made his way to the front.

All was quiet. Even the afflicted girls ceased their gibbering when Reverend Johnson came into the room.

He was not alone. He had another one with him. Not Elias Cornwell, who had stationed himself next to the afflicted girls, but someone no one had seen before. Except me.

I watched in a trance, as if scrying my own past, as Obadiah Wilson mounted the pulpit. He moved slowly, holding on to the rail that winds up the side of it. He stood at the top, knuckles white on the rounded balustrade. I knew it was him, even though his hair was thinner, his pale face had withered, and fever spots showed high on his drawn cheeks. And he knew me. He looked over the heads of all those gathered in front of him, pale eyes questing, until he found me. He began to speak then but was suddenly overcome with coughing. He stopped his mouth with his handkerchief. He took it away, the white linen spotted bright with blood, and began again.

"There is one among you . . ." His voice was low and hoarse, pitched only a little above a whisper, like corn husks rubbing together, but it rang around the hall like a clarion call. "There is one among you who comes as a wolf among sheep. There is one among you who bears the mark of the beast!"

He stood, black arm extended, his bony finger pointing straight at me.

His thin chest heaved as he took in breath to say more, but Hannah had already risen from her place.

She had not spoken a coherent sentence since the beginning of her affliction. Now she was shouting:

"Mary! It is Mary! She comes to me in spirit!"

Cries went up round the hall.

"She speaks! She speaks!"

"The spell is broken!"

"Praise be the Lord!"

Then they all rose up, all the other girls together, and called with one voice:

"Mary! Mary! Mary!" They turned, pointing where Obadiah Wilson's finger was pointing. "Mary! Mary! Mary!"

"Does she bring another with her?" Obadiah Wilson's voice whispered, insistent, down from the pulpit.

"She brings the Devil with her! She bids me write in his book!" Hannah answered. Suddenly she yelped, as if pinched or stung. Her face contorted and her hands raked her body, scratching, pulling at her clothes. "She afflicts me! She sends herself against me! Don't, Mary! Don't, Mary!"

"Don't, Mary! Don't, Mary!" They all began to shake and shudder, like puppets strung together. "She shadows me! I freeze! I freeze!"

The Reverend Cornwell stepped forward, touching one girl after another.

"They are cold!" His tone was one of wonder. "'Tis true! 'Tis true!"

"Now she is a bird!" Hannah waved her hands toward the rafters. "See how she flies! She flies!"

The girls stared up as one, necks straining, heads weaving back and forth as though following a fluttering movement only they could see.

Obadiah Wilson needed no more.

"Seize her! Bring her to me!"

His hoarse voice rasped the order and Reverend Johnson signalled to the tithing men standing at the door. They stepped forward to take me, but the place was descending into uproar. All around, people were rising, jostling each other to see what was happening. Girls were crying out from all over the room, flailing about, falling and fainting. I ducked down, dodging elbows, stepping over the bench, to get to the back of the room. Tobias had seen me. He left his place on the men's benches and lifted the bar on the door. I slipped out under his arm, and the door shut behind me. I heard him slide the bar back and saw the door bulge as he settled his bulk against it.

I have taken refuge in Rebekah's borning room. Rebekah is near her time, very near. Martha says they will not dare to enter here. Sarah has brought me what I asked for: food, boy's clothing, a blanket. I take the moccasins and the little leather pouch from my box and put the pouch round my neck. My few precious things. All I have to show for my life so far lived. All I have to take with me to the wilderness. I must take my chances there. If I stay here, I hang for sure. I want to stay. I want to see the baby safe delivered. Rebekah's birth pains come closer together; it will not be long now, but I can stay no longer. Martha hovers like a frightened bird and

Mary's diary ends here.

*testimony*

These pages, written in a different hand, were found in the borders of the quilt.

I am an unlettered woman, but I feel beholden to keep faith with Mary and finish her story (what I know of it).

She wanted to stay, but had no choice but for to go. They came straight from the Meeting House, guessing rightly that she would run like a vixen to her own home cover. We did what we could for her by way of food and clothing that would be fitting, for the nights were getting bitter cold and she was heading for wilderness parts.

They came in deputation, Reverend Johnson and Elias Cornwell along with Nathaniel Clench and the constables and a crowd of others. John Rivers and Tobias stood ready with musket and sword, but Sarah forbade them to fight.

She and John told them that Mary has been and gone.

John and Sarah are well-respected, Sarah is well-connected to several leading families, and never a stain to her name. John likewise. The constables stood all undecided, looking to Nathaniel Clench at the head of them, as he and Sarah are related. Under his direction they would have gone away. But Reverend Johnson steps forward and orders them to search the place.

"Search all you like," Sarah says to Johnson. "She's not here."

They did search, both houses, from eaves to root cellar. All except the borning room. They found nothing. So they come back again, demanding to enter where no man should be.

"You'll not pass." I stepped forward. "Not with him at any rate." They had a stranger with them. A withered stick of a man, coughing and spluttering blood into his kerchief. The mark of death is upon him. He ain't long for this world. "He has the coughing sickness, like as not consumption. Would you have him breathe infection on a newborn? Go your ways, masters. There's work to do here. Women's work. When the babe is born and safe away, you can search all you want."

I stood before them, hands bloodied. Behind me Rebekah was screaming in pain in good and earnest. The men flinched back, as well they might. Tobias stepped up, John with him. They stood before the door, shoulder to shoulder. To get in, the men would have to go through them.

They went away, warning that they would be back.

Tobias stood guard until morning. By then the baby had come, and Mary was gone. John Rivers offered her his horse but she refused it, saying that where she was going, a horse would be next to useless. He did what he could, seeing her safe out of the village and into the forest. From there she went on alone.

Rebekah's had a girl child. She names her Mary Sarah, but the child will not be baptized here.

We are leaving, as soon as may be. Now the crying out has started, it will not stop. Cheated of one, they will go for others. Me and Jonah, like as not. I don't reckon much on our chances, what with him a stranger and me a healer, and Jonah is inclined to agree. They might stay off John and Sarah, for a while at least, because of their standing, but there's never any telling. Many a woman of wealth and position has swung from the gallows tree. Jonah is packing the wagon; we will go as soon as he has finished.

Sarah and John will come on with Rebekah and Tobias, as soon as Rebekah is well enough to travel. I counsel *no delay*.

She showed me where her writings were hid, and as I scribe this, I sew it in with the rest. When we leave, I will take her box and this quilt in it. One day, mayhap, she will find us, and she can take back her story. Until that day comes, I will keep all safe. Then she will know how I kept faith.

We depart for Salem, no one stopping us, but think to go south from there. Jonah has heard of places where folk are freer to follow their own conscience, which is one of the reasons we crossed over the ocean in the first place. We will leave word for her, each place we go.

CELIA REES is the author of many novels for teens. She writes full-time and lives in England with her husband, Terry; their daughter, Catrin; and their cat, Poppy.